T0343647

BERLIN

by Andris Kupriss

Translated by Ian Gwin

Curated by Kaija Straumanis as part of the 2025 Translator Triptych

OPEN LETTER
LITERARY TRANSLATIONS FROM THE UNIVERSITY OF ROCHESTER

Originally published as *Berlīne* by Orbita, 2019
Copyright © Andris Kuprišs, 2019
Translation copyright © Ian Gwin, 2025

First edition, 2025
All rights reserved.

Library of Congress Cataloging-in-Publication data: Available.
ISBN (pb): 978-1-960385-14-7 | ISBN (ebook): 978-1-960385-21-5

This project is supported in part by an award from the National Endowment for the Arts.

This project is also made possible by the New York State Council on the Arts with the
support of the Office of the Governor and the New York State Legislature.

Cover design by Jenny Volvovski

Published by Open Letter at the University of Rochester
Morey 303, Rochester, NY 14627
www.openletterbooks.org

Printed on permanent/durable acid-free paper in Canada

BERLIN

CONTENTS

PROLETARIAN THERAPY

You might have walked right past the place, located somewhere on the outskirts of the city: a two-story building off the main road with a small pub. Kept out of sight by tall trees, a narrow asphalt path leads to a cellar where a jasmine tree grows by the door.

Even though it was winter and the branches were bare, you still needed to know exactly where the place was to find it. But I knew where I was going, and why. It could have been a Friday or Saturday; the bar was packed. I saw right away that the only person more attractive than me was the bartender. With its really long, wooden benches—the kind you always find in bars—the room felt more narrow than it was despite the pool table in the center. I went straight for the bar, but no one was behind it so I turned around to assess the situation, find a spot to sit. All the tables were taken. Some people were standing, others playing pool. When I turned around again, the bartender was looking at me. Her hair was dyed a scarlet red and her plunging neckline revealed dry skin, desiccated over years. Her stare was direct and level to mine. And it surprised me, because there was something other than the usual "What do you want?" in it, something more gentle and inviting. I decided to speak, but she spoke first.

"Your eyes are red. Have you been crying?"

I thought about it, but couldn't remember.

"Honey, don't sweat it! Whatever's going on, you'll get through it. Maybe a girl? But don't worry, it'll all work out!"

I went quiet and tried to think over what she'd said. Then I began to think of how I might answer.

"What can I get you?" she asked.

I ordered beer and pistachios, and out of the corner of my eye noticed a little table with two chairs off to the corner, by the bathroom.

"Take a seat, I'll be back in a few minutes," she said. I nodded.

I found a seat comfortably out of the way, where I could see nearly the entire bar. This proved useful, as the mood soon took a turn for the worst—a fight broke out. Judging by the general level of drunkenness, it could have been three or four in the mourning. Whatever the two men were loudly screaming about, why some women were shouting, why the pool players kept calmly lining up shots, why the bartender cussed the two of them out at the bar, threatening to call the police, even though everyone knew the police wouldn't come, why exactly the first and only punch came, right fist to nose, which immediately began to gush unimaginable amounts of blood, pouring over the guy's shirt, why this didn't alarm me in the slightest, I don't know. I was still thinking over what I had said to the bartender earlier, had even started to doubt if I'd heard her correctly, and wondered if she had been hitting on me ambiguously. Meanwhile the blood was being cleaned off the tile floor, and pressing questions could be heard as—who's the asshole who, and are you the son of a bitch that—along with future proposals, how both might meet again to fully resolve their mutual relationship questions.

Eventually the bartender took a seat at my table, setting a half-finished glass of grapefruit juice down on it.

"Your eyes are really red. They look pretty bad. But honey, don't worry. I see people like you every day. They come in, complain about life . . ."

Right then I wanted to interrupt, say I wasn't complaining about anything, but I didn't have a chance.

"But there's something strange about you. You're not from here. I've never seen you before. First time?"

I wanted to answer, but missed my chance again.

"Honey, believe me. I don't know what's going on, whatever's not right in your young life. But I'm sure everything will be alright, no need to cry. And if this girl—and I know it's a girl—she doesn't deserve another fucking tear from you. You hear me, honey? But if you're here because someone died—oh, why cry about it? I left, you won't return. Christ, your eyes are so red!"

Suddenly she went silent. I decided to wait for her to continue, or see if she expected an answer from me, but then I realized she didn't expect anything from me at all. She sat there, facing the room, perhaps assessing whether another fight would break out. A man was tottering toward the bar.

"I need to get back to work," she said, then stood up. I sat there for a little while, finished my beer, poured the rest of the pistachios into my coat pocket, and left.

THE APOLOGY

I remember one lesson cost fifteen lats. So the whole course cost something like forty, even sixty lats, total. I don't how much my father's wages were at the time. Maybe two-hundred. Or closer to three-hundred. All I know was how badly I wanted to take the course. My dad knew too, which is why he agreed to pay for it. I was twelve or thirteen at the time. I knew our family couldn't afford such an expensive course, but we budgeted for it, because I really, really wanted to go. I didn't press them. I knew how much it would cost. But my dad agreed because he knew how important it was to me. Lessons were once a week, on Tuesdays, I think. Or maybe Wednesdays. Now I remember, lessons were Wednesdays for sure; I know because while writing they were on Tuesdays it came to me that they actually were on Wednesdays, because them being on Wednesdays plays an important part in what happens later. And so when I remembered what took place before, I also remembered it was Wednesdays, because both my father and I say the word "Wednesday" in the conversation that happens later, meaning sometime—some day of the week—after I wanted to attend this course and my father agreed to pay for it. But the conversation is really important. Honestly, the conversation was the first thing I recalled, and why I started writing this in the first place.

After the first lesson, the organizer came up to me and asked if I had ever done anything like this before. I told him no. He looked surprised, since from a distance it looked like I knew what I was doing, while I was actually doing it for the first time in my life. I was, apparently, a natural. I felt flattered, happy. Something had come naturally to me. I excelled at something. And given that everyone else in the course was much older than me, I was all the happier. I was the youngest, but what we were taught came easiest to me.

The second or third lesson was that particular Wednesday. In the morning, as per usual, I was at school, but afterward I went straight to the course, which was a fifteen-minute walk from school, or twenty minutes from home. Most of the time after coming home from school I would drop off my bag, eat, then walk to the course. It was really important to my dad that I ate. Cooked food was always ready and waiting for me at home—peeled potatoes, soaked in water and left on the stove, as well as a second meal in the fridge—pre-cooked chicken strips or pork cutlets. All I had to do was light the burner and reheat the food on the pan. Dad always had stomach trouble; all his health problems seemed to stem from the stomach. It was very important to him that I eat regular, healthy meals, because I'd had stomach problems as a young child. He was insistent on this, and would get upset with me when he came home from work only to hear that I hadn't eaten anything that day. He got really aggravated and his anger scared me, however nuanced its manifestations were: just a look, or a few words even; later a raised voice—but never physical violence. That's why I got good at faking meals, boiling the potatoes and greasing the pan so it looked like I'd eaten, though I hadn't touched a bite. Most of the time I took food with me, and when I met up with friends after school I'd throw it in the bushes, since my parents would count the cutlets and potatoes, I thought, and I had to get rid of them so they'd believe I had eaten.

The third lesson was that Wednesday; maybe I'd had to stay after school for some reason, because I chose to go straight to the course instead of stopping at home. The lesson lasted a few hours, and aside from that I had to consider the time it took to get there. I'm not sure if I got good marks at school that day, but I do know that afterward I made my way home without a care in the world. It was late afternoon, warm, I think, but not yet summer—it couldn't have been summer, school is out then. Writing this I'm beginning to doubt I had been at school that morning before going to the course, because maybe it was summer and school was over, but the first part of the day, most likely, I had walked down from Kolkasraga Street to Imanta Street, where I spent so many days of my childhood and adolescence sitting outside with Dad, taking apart, cleaning, oiling, and putting back together the rear assemblies of our bicycles. In all likelihood we hadn't even assembled them correctly, or some part of the bikes had broken down from wear, since I kind of doubted then whether we could fix those Soviet-built objects. Now I'm left with the impression that of course I could disassemble the rear spokes and put them together again. Still, I often had issues with the bike, since the chain would grow loose, and since I couldn't fix that I would let it go, though sometimes it didn't break lose and the whole bike worked fine.

It was late spring, on a Wednesday, when I had to walk to the third lesson. For the first part of the day I was in school, the air was warm, flowers in bloom maybe, because after school when we walked Kolkasraga Street by way of Imanta Street there were so many bushes flowering outside the houses on Imanta. When it was time to go to lessons I realized I wouldn't have a chance to stop at home to drop off my bag and eat, so I turned from Kolkasraga onto Bezdelīga Street, where the course was held, and afterward walked home on that still-warm, late spring evening. Nothing particular happened that day, so I was in a good mood—in any case I definitely felt good, at least compared with how I felt once I got home.

Everything happened quickly, mercilessly. I didn't have time to put down my bag or even take off my shoes, because as soon as I got through the door my father was standing before me. He was angry like never before; maybe he yelled, though I can remember him yelling at full volume only once before. I couldn't have been but a few years old, and Mom had to bring me with her somewhere and forgot to tell him beforehand that we wouldn't be home until late, and so he didn't know where we were and when we finally got home he was really upset and shouted at her for a while. Furious, he paced back and forth over the old, gray-green carpet in the front hall, while Mom lay in bed, pressing a damp compress to her forehead, the kind she made using his handkerchiefs; I gathered she had a headache, because in our house that was the only way to deal with them.

She didn't say a word, just lay there pressing the compress down harder while dad yelled about how irresponsibly she had dealt with things, how she hadn't called him, hadn't left a note in the usual place on the kitchen table. He shouted in Russian— which means this took place pre-1994, the year he agreed with my mother to speak only Latvian, whereas until then (and for all my life) he'd spoken Russian with her. One word of my father's monologue stands out in my memory: Ведьма. He must have been truly upset because I had never heard him say that before. He almost never swore, and the only time I remember him doing so was when he yelled.

That Wednesday, when I got back home after the course, I walked into our house on Sabile Street, where Dad was waiting, angry. He didn't ask any questions, just started to yell and swear at me. I was surprised, and wasn't even ready to defend myself. "Where have you been?" he asked. I wanted to respond, but he didn't give me a chance. He accused me of being irresponsible, reproached me for being reckless. How I left in the morning only to come home now, without calling, without any word. And on a Wednesday, too, when you have those lessons, he said, but are your lessons today? But they are today . . . I forgot all about that—what an idiot! And as he spoke I stood there, trying to pull myself together. If, unconsciously, I had been locked into some automatic awareness of guilt, then now there was one thing I had in my defense. "I was at lessons," I said quietly, "I was at lessons and came home."

It was Wednesday, a hot summer afternoon, hot like in Southern Europe, and I had just come inside. In the kitchen, potatoes and cutlets were cooking on the stovetop. Dad was listening to me, and stood there stiffly. At that moment there were probably a thousand thoughts running through his mind about what he'd done and what was happening here. He was confused. Not ready to stand down, though no longer on the attack. I walked past him and toward my room. I was also confused, since I was hurt by his empty anger. It the worst feeling I'd ever experienced. Dad disappeared into the bathroom. Not a second later he came out, approached me, his eyes inflamed with summer heat, and said, softly: "Please, son, forgive me!" Then he stepped outside for a walk in the August afternoon, where the summer grows cool and the leaves, warmed by the sun, warn that Autumn soon will come.

YOU'RE THE FIRST PERSON
I'VE TOLD

Gustavs was happy to accept an invitation from his instructor to come visit. I wouldn't say the two were friends, but they'd met a few times downtown—the first time when everyone went to a posh bar to drink Guinness and talk about brewing techniques and the taste of particular beers. His instructor had noted the sourness of certain Belgian beers, while Gustavs had talked about what makes the production of white wine different from red. With pride he brought up how, while still only sixteen years old, he had won a lifestyle magazine's wine trivia competition by answering that very question, whether you can turn white wine into red. Gustavs had read that red wine gets its color from the skin of the grapes, and so if you separate these from the mix, any wine will retain the light tint it starts out with. As a prize, Gustavs received an invitation to an official lunch with the jury.

A few weeks later they met again, and went out to dinner. The teacher chose the restaurant, and Gustavs, knowing how fancy it would be, decided to dress accordingly. That night he put on his father's dark-gray suit and one of his old ties. His father and mother watched him from their room as he inspected himself in the mirror of their old, two-story flat. After a few attempts he successfully knotted the tie, just like his father had taught him. It pleased him to see a fully grown man in the mirror. Gustavs felt good in the suit coat, though it was cut too large for him. He was an attentive son, and though able to discern little details and taste seemingly minor, yet significant differences, he failed to notice the smiles and mocking looks of the restaurant staff while he and the teacher asked for one of the better tables by a window with a view to one of the small, fenced-in gardens of old-town Riga. He failed, too, to hear the tinge of sarcasm in the voice of the waitress who came to serve the two gentlemen. Instead he took sips of the red wine (which Gustavs had chosen) and tasted the shrimp salad (which the teacher picked out). He'd never tried shrimp salad before, and it tasted great, mostly because it had so much mayonnaise. That time they talked mostly about German, and also the teacher's experience living in Berlin.

The third time they met, the instructor invited Gustavs over to his home. The instructor opened the door dressed in the same clothes he wore every day to German lessons—a threadbare but well-cut blazer and mismatched slacks. His sunny, spacious apartment smelled like incense. It could have been as large as five rooms, but Gustavs didn't have the chance to look, since his host had already shown him into the sitting-room. Gustavs passed by a window and glanced outside. It was the weekend, and only a few people stood along the street next to the tram station. He fancied to himself whether any of them were nearly as interesting as he was this Saturday. Returning from the kitchen, the instructor was talking about how, aside from him, an older gentleman also lived in the apartment and sometimes sublet one of the rooms for a few months. Gustavs noticed a plate of fish beside slices of cheese and grapes left on the coffee table, while at the edge of the dresser he saw a three-liter box of wine with a small, black spigot. The instructor had brought it back from a trip, supposedly, and left it open. Some guests had drunk most of it the night before, though a few liters were left—they filled the glasses which the instructor held out.

Their conversation began with the appreciation of wine. Gustavs sat in an armchair, while the teacher sat on a small couch across from him. Again Gustavs brought up winning the wine contest, and just how surprised the organizers appeared when they saw someone so young turn up at the official lunch. Gustavs had been somewhat disappointed that none of the founding editors or participants in the contest were ready to have a serious conversation about wine with him—though he wouldn't have been able to say much, Gustavs now admitted, because he only knew what he'd read—but they were ready to talk about other subjects, not only wine but the finer things in life, like cuisine or cigars, and though he'd never smoked any cigars he wished he could talk about them, as he seldom had the chance to talk about finer things, only banal things, what his friends are interested in, but they aren't interested in cigars or wine at all, if they were it would probably be some cheap swill to get drunk on, and that didn't interest Gustavs, who hoped to savor and appreciate the taste, and why he took so much pride in winning the contest that round, and also why he was so disappointed in the end that, even though the lunch went well and the two types of wine given to attendees to try—a white and a red—tasted fine, they seemed somewhat expensive at six or seven lats a bottle—his parents would never buy that kind, they didn't really drink wine, Dad said it tasted sour, and besides he wasn't particularly enthused with Gustavs's passion for wine, as seventeen was a little young to be interested in alcohol, though Mom said there was something to celebrate in reading about wine and beginning to learn about its culture—and yet Gustavs was disappointed by the lunch, feeling uncomfortable in the company of adults who most likely didn't feel all that comfortable in the company of such an improper young aficionado, which was why, after waiting around, as some grapes and sweet fruits were offered, he declined and politely said goodbye, shook hands with the senior editor, and left.

The teacher listened carefully to Gustavs, observing him and asking here and there whether he could refill his glass. After two glasses of red wine, Gustavs began to feel warm and talkative. He wondered to himself how long he'd been in the apartment, maybe an hour and a half or more, at least, while the teacher merely looked on with his usual expression, which Gustavs viewed as an explicit interest in what he was talking about, a goodwill which he had never encountered from an adult before, the kind of goodwill which asks for nothing in return, which you feel supported by. He felt a kinship with the teacher, that they were cut from the same cloth. Gustavs felt as though his instructor meant well, that he could discern fine wine and cheese, unlike the people at the tram stop, who didn't know about the finer things in life, but Gustavs did, all he needed was to acquire them. Gustavs also knew a third was a glass too many, but didn't refuse when the teacher offered. As he watched the teacher rise, approach the dresser, and begin to pour some wine from the spigot on a small black box of wine, he heard the front door unlock and saw a tall man with a nondescript expression appear in the living room door. The man was silent for a moment or two. Still in his chair, Gustavs turned away from him. The teacher held out two full glasses. He, too, had turned away from the man. A red drop had taken shape under the spigot on the black box of wine, and without anyone noticing, fell soundlessly, dissolving onto the parquet floor. Though he'd been sitting with his back to the window, Gustavs suddenly realized it was already dark out. He knew then that he had been in the apartment for over four hours.

The teacher spoke first and explained to the man who had entered that Gustavs was one of his students. "Er spricht Deutsch," he said, smiling. "Ach so?" the man asked, smiling as well. "Nur ein bisschen," Gustavs said, blushing, and instinctively looked for his glass, still in the teacher's hand. The man gave Gustavs a cool, if not unironic once over. Then he turned and without a word walked into the next room and shut the door.

Gustavs got home on time. His parents were sitting in easy chairs watching television, as usual. He went to his room and began to change. From the other room his father asked how the visit went. Gustavs got into bed and opened a book on wine. He thought back to the apartment, the incense, and the people at the tram stop who hadn't resolved to learn about the finer things in life. He thought about the strange man, his teacher, and whether he could ever call the teacher his friend.

THE REFUSAL

I finally worked up the courage to go, even though I was sure I could find some reason to refuse the generous host of the party, a best friend of mine. After everything that had happened in the last few months, I had no desire to take part in any social event, to meet young people, listen to them talk about their work and their hobbies, join in conversations about politics, the price of real estate or the national status of Rietumu Banka. But I was hard pressed for a truly good excuse, and also knew my friend would be offended if I didn't show up.

There were already a lot of people there when I arrived; the time had come when everyone's formed various groups separated by interest, age, or however long they've known each other. I was offered wine, took some, and with glass in hand set sail through the apartment, drifting from this group to that, listening to conversations without interjecting. A few times the hostess approached me to say how glad she was I could make it, then refilled my glass with red wine. Once I had stood by each clique for long enough, I decided to find a quiet corner.

I wasn't bored, the wine kept me warm, but even that wasn't enough to douse some lingering thoughts I would have rather not been dwelling on. Truthfully, the wish to cast them aside, even partially, was partly why I had decided to come.

While wandering the apartment, I walked into a home office or small library. There was a large writing desk piled high with papers, documents, notes, and stacks of books; I knew the hostess's husband was a writer, or journalist, or blogger, or something like that, though I had read none of his books, his essays, or his blog posts. Quite smart and talented, people told me. I agreed. As I ambled by the shelves, I noticed Kafka and Borges, a contemporary Norwegian writer who I also hadn't read, though people told me he was brilliant. I agreed.

"Bored too?"

I turned around and saw, standing in the door to the office, a young woman. I had noticed her talking with one clique, but then later another; by the looks of it she had taken the same tactic, keeping company without seeking anything concrete, merely whiling away the time.

"You're drinking red wine," she said, more as a statement than any kind of question. I couldn't tell if she regarded that positively, or if the glass in my hand testified to some lack in my character.

I made a clumsy joke in response, she laughed quietly, and after that we sat down on the office couch, and our conversation turned out to be pretty interesting, but maybe that was the wine talking. Twice I went to fetch a new bottle, and still another time I failed to notice how attentively, a little impolitely, even, I stared at her in that black dress, her shoulders, her fingernails, and lips as she spoke about her trip to Budapest with her former fiancé. At the word *former* I leaned in, closer— maybe because she pronounced it with a certain emphasis, a certain tact, but that could have just been how I perceived it; in all likelihood, the wine had gotten to me. And though the word stuck in my head, I didn't ask, yet as it turned out I didn't need to ask, because she had, most likely, sensed a need to now emphasize her fiancé as former, since not long after they returned from Budapest he left her, as he had different plans and priorities, and yet how stupid did he have to be, I thought, to leave this woman for priorities.

One by one people had been stopping into the office where we sat, looking for someone, or asking if we had seen one guest or another; we nodded and smiled, showing off our wine-stained teeth. We both knew where this was taking us, so we slowed down on the drinking. Dawn came, people went, the apartment took on a peaceful hush, the sun shone, and the moment of departure was approaching. Finally we got up from the couch and went into the living room. Embers from last night smoldered ever so quietly in the fireplace, and just as quietly I heard she had to get home. At that moment, in the living room where we stood, a mirror reflected her cobalt lips, she had already called a taxi, it was waiting outside, she said I could give you a ride home, and I think there's half a bottle of wine at my place, and I don't need to go to sleep right away, and though I'd been waiting for that moment nearly all night long, something in me had transformed, maybe it was the morning light, beaming through the white curtains, which reminded me again of the single thought I had successfully kept under wraps this whole time, and I knew then I wouldn't be putting my coat on, wouldn't be sharing her taxi, because I knew what came next; of course, I'd already imagined how we'd arrive at her place: a bottle of wine waiting for us on the table, but we wouldn't even touch it and we'd come to our senses in her bed, which smells like another man, but, what's worse, while I carefully undress her—first the black dress, then the minimal, yet elegant lingerie—it's not her exquisite figure that's on my mind, but another, far more familiar one; and what my eyes desire will be the ruin of my hands, for hands remember better than sight or sound, and when I caress her, cup her breasts, slowly trace her hips, my hands will quickly grow numb, without getting to know what I longed for so badly in this other body, and when she lifts her hips so I can take off my pants, my eyes are joined to my hands, because even they don't notice what they've been waiting for; they know what they want to see, but the sight of this will be something different entirely, even the smell different, and all five senses rage against me, my heart starts, and humiliation comes and then disappointment, looks of confusion, and uneasy misunderstandings.

That's how it might go, I realize, and my companion that night knew immediately from the look on my face; maybe the same thing happened to her before, and that's why she wasn't offended, but merely kissed me goodbye and hurried out to take a taxi home to a bed smelling so intimate, to finish off the last of that bottle, to cry a while and fall asleep on the living room couch, because she hasn't slept in the bed since her fiancé left.

Meanwhile, I'll be the last one at the party, last to go out onto the balcony and light a cigarette; my partner will come up and hug me from behind, rest her head on my shoulder and, with a smile and smelling a little like wine, hold me tight and ask, without raising her head:

"How are you?"

THE RAPE

A key slid in the lock and turned. She was tired and though she'd gone to bed on time she couldn't fall asleep; she tossed and turned, dreamt about numbers, addition problems she had to solve, but she couldn't come up with the right answer and didn't really know what she was supposed to come up with. One number added up with another and each time she knew the sum wasn't right; it annoyed and upset her enough to keep her from sleep. Her head ached, and heat of the radiator made the room stifling. The sound of the key in the lock actually made her glad; it interrupted her continual counting. Then he came in; she heard him quietly shut the door, not turning on the light for fear of waking her. She liked little gestures like that. She didn't stir or turn her head to look and watch him entering the apartment where she was, once again, living alone. And though her sleep had been irregular, she didn't feel for her phone to look at the time, didn't stir or open her eyes, only listened to the key slide in and turn twice in the lock, the door open, him entering the apartment. She lay there with her face to the wall, listening to him take off his shoes, come into the room, begin to undress. He took off his winter coat first, undid the buttons of his shirt, took off his pants and socks. She heard him pull off his underwear, throw the clothes into a pile on the floor, like he did whenever he undressed in the dark before crawling in next to her under the covers. His skin hadn't touched hers, but she could already feel the chill of the street on him; his skin hadn't touched hers, but he could already feel her warmth under the covers. She waited for him to get close, but all he did was lie down next to her, his face against her back, and hold his breath to hear whether she was asleep. Just lying there: she, expecting him to snuggle up to her—he, wondering if his touch hadn't woken her. He didn't want to wake her. Finally, he took her in his arms, very carefully, feeling her back, warm against his cold abdomen. His shoulders were colder, but he didn't want to brush her with his feet, which would tickle.

"I can't sleep."

"I know. You're awake."

Touching his nose to the back of her head.

"It's me," he said

"I know. It's you. What time is it?"

"Sometime."

"What time is it?"

"A little after three."

Moving his hand under her arm, taking her left breast in his palm.

"Hey."

"Hey."

She, thinking how she needed to fall asleep so she could get at least a few hours of rest; he, thinking how he'd gotten there later than he would have liked, which didn't really leave a lot of time.

She let out a barely audible groan—a sign she was feeling safe.

"I'd like to get a little sleep."

"I'd like you to sleep with me a little."

Then they were quiet. Closing her eyes, she tried to fall asleep, thinking instead of how long his smell would linger in the sheets. Opening his eyes, he looked out the window. From that angle, he saw only the still branches of a tree; beyond, the clouds moved scarlet by the nocturnal light of city streets. The sheets were piled on thick, so after a while he started to sweat; she'd warmed him from the chill of the empty street. He must have dozed off because he heard a key slide in the lock and turn. Then, listening, he heard the door open. He turned his head toward it and held his breath.

"You're awake," she said.

"I can't fall asleep."

"What are you thinking of?"

"Someone coming through the door. Sometimes I think the door gets left unlocked."

For a moment they were silent, listening. No one was coming.

"You can go and check," she said.

"I locked it."

He turned back and caught sight of her face. She turned to him, then hooked a leg over his hip.

"Hey," he whispered.

"Hey."

"I think I dozed off. Someone opened the door and came in and then closed it, but it must have been a dream. The room needed rearranging, except I would put something in a new place just to turn around again and find everything back where it was. It was so frustrating I started to cry, but I felt ashamed about crying and woke up."

"What time is it?"

He looked at the window.

"Half past four."

She pressed her nose to his chest.

"We don't have to talk about this," she said from under the covers.

"Tell me how it happened. We won't be sleeping tonight anyways."

"Why do you want to hear it?"

Again she turned her back to him and pressed herself against him.

"I want to touch you," he said.

"Touch me, please."

He put his hand on her stomach, sliding it lower. With his fingers he found her hip bones and felt them. He brushed her left leg, his fingers sliding down to her shin, then back up, his fingertips resting just above her knees.

"You were away when it happened. He was already drunk when he got here, the door was unlocked that night. At first I wanted to tell him to leave, but he insisted he had something important to tell me. He asked me to pour him a drink, so I let him have the last of the whiskey from my birthday. We sat in the kitchen until I finally said something, that it was time for him to get going, but he just sat there, listening and slowly drinking. I said he had to hurry up because you were coming home soon, and he said I had nothing to worry about because he knew that night you weren't."

He had stopped caressing her and was sweating again.

"He took my arms like this and pulled me to him. I wasn't even frightened at first. I just thought: I'm such an idiot. I mean, how could this happen? I thought you were coming through the door, but you weren't. He pushed me onto the table, tore off my skirt, getting on top of me. I didn't cry out, or scream, I just kicked him as much as I could, scratched him with my nails. But he couldn't feel at all, like he was more drunk than I'd thought, but like, he was totally drunk, beyond numb. His eyes were bright, cloudy, but he was still stronger than me. He held me down by the hair on the table so I couldn't get up. When I tried he pulled my hair again, it hurt so much I blacked out for a second. I tried to clamp my legs shut, but he just pulled me by the hair, pushed my knees apart and undid his pants. I didn't cry out, or scream, I just thought of how you still weren't here, why it was him and not you who came through the door that night. I thought, I'm waiting for you but then he came, and I'm such an idiot, I let him in and now he's raping me and might not even remember tomorrow morning."

He rolled onto his back and looked out the window again. She fell silent. He held his breath to hear if she was crying in the stifling room, but she was completely silent. He was the one who felt like crying.

"You know, it's still in me, that tenderness," she said after a while. "But someday, I think, it will pass, disappear—that feeling, that tenderness. But it won't go away, it'll always be there. Sometimes I think of how long it can live inside me. And it scares me. I was glad about that feeling before, but now I'm scared. It's like an infection eating away inside me, a parasite keeping its host alive in order to consume it. That tenderness . . . it's the most fragile thing in the world, I think. One stupid thing is all it takes for it to crumble. Then it sits there, smoldering, hungry. It'll be a long time before I feed it again. Until I die? That would be torture. I don't believe in that kind of cruelty. But even now, I'm afraid. As a kid I was told not to cry after I lost my first tooth, since a new one would grow in its place. But that didn't really help me. Then, when I'd grown a bit and had adult teeth, I started to get cavities and had to get my first filling. I asked how long it would have to stay in and was told forever. I didn't understand—forever. Well if not forever, then for a long time. But as a kid I didn't know the difference between forever and a long time. And I cried because it was the first time something was damaged for the rest of my life. Stupid, isn't it?"

"It's not stupid."

Now he knew that, luckily, he wouldn't cry, and cuddled back up to her. He grasped her breast with his palm. She whimpered.

"This isn't going to go away, is it? We have to accept it?"

He placed his hand on her warm stomach.

"He called the next morning. Spent a long time apologizing, crying loudly into the receiver, wailing, asking if I'd forgive him, saying he'd had no clue he was capable of anything like that, it had never happened before, saying he couldn't explain his behavior. We both cried and cried. But you already know everything that happened after that."

"I know."

"And I didn't feel guilty, I didn't feel ashamed, that's the main thing. I was just really sorry. So, so, sorry, that for days after I just cried and felt sorry for myself, and for him. At times I got so angry and so upset that I stopped crying altogether, but when I was no longer upset, that tenderness resurfaced. I felt sorry for myself. It was him. He came in, not you: you were supposed to be there. Because I was waiting for you, but he came."

"It's not my fault," he said.

"It's not your fault."

"Turn over. Look at me, please."

Without wanting to, she turned to him and looked.

"Hey."

"Hey."

"What time is it?"

She looked out the window.

"Nearly six."

"I have to go soon. I need to get back out before the streets get busy. Otherwise I'll be seen and reported. They wouldn't like that."

"No, they wouldn't. You're going?"

"I'm going, but in a minute. I'm going to touch you."

"Touch me, please." And she turned her head, and he snuggled close to her. She could feel the sweat on his body.

"Could you sing for me a little," she whispered, closing her eyes.

He looked out the window at the still branches. Then he began to sing, his lips close to her ear: "Drüben hinterm Dorfe steht ein Leiermann." She felt his chest vibrating. "Und mit starren Fingern dreht er, was er kann." They both heard the melody, moving slower for him, with more emphasis in the pauses; for her somewhat more quickly, lighter. Then he was quiet again. He held his breath to hear if she had fallen asleep.

"What time is it?" he asked.

THE LAST WALK
BEFORE BEGINNING

Finally, I remembered. That night of first frost, when every-thing—ground, pavement, trees and bushes—was sheathed in sheer white, a pure dusting of crystal ice. I was the first to step over that purity, to be guilty of leaving footprints on white ground. I walked for a while, there was no one else was around. Only railroad tracks, tramlines, blank factory walls, and quiet streets of wooden houses. How lucky I was, I thought, to be alone in such emptiness. I needed to get home, and yet there I lingered. As I walked on, the delicate beauty of the winter night inspired me with ambitions so grand I could never start them, and even while my thoughts were clouded, due to the sharpening of my melancholy afflictions, I gradually realized how lucky I was, then; how a walk in the snow felt like one last meal before an execution, so I didn't run or fear that some adversary could be waiting around the corner of that famous building, waiting to thrust a pocket knife between my ribs, punishment for the sum of my transgressions during the last two and a half years at least, but by the time I made it to the corner I was ready for him, and first I threw a punch toward the vacant railroad station, telling myself what I crime I had just committed. I was speaking Latvian, apparently, but shortly as I returned to the corner where I would have to wait to see the face of my adversary, no one was there, and then I understood that I had no other choice but to go home, lay in bed, and wait for everything to begin.

A TYPICAL FIT OF MELANCHOLY: A CASE STUDY

It often begins at dawn. Between the blinds, blue light—our introduction to the fit, a prelude, if you will. Picture a mind enshrouded in mist, where thoughts thick and dense agglomerate. One, weightier than all the rest, weans itself away, only to push on remorselessly for the fit's remaining duration. An attack may last, on average, between twenty-four to thirty-six hours.

The patient remains alone with that solitary thought; it forecloses sleep. He experiences diffuse hallucinations, along with various songs, fragments of melodies, which ceaselessly play in his head like radio transmissions which he's unable to turn down or off. It's vital to note how insomnia is a primary symptom of the melancholic attack—however fervently the patient desires or even pleads for rest, the disease refuses him. To the contrary, melancholy does everything in its power to make him feel each and every nuance of a debilitation and decay. It could be argued that this expresses the very essence of melancholia—its ethos, one could venture.

Arguments have been made that the true source of melancholic attacks is poetry (from the Ancient Greek "poiesis"—"to create"). In such cases, the patient lacks the mental capacity to differentiate poetic personas, resulting in neurotic conditions during which poetically-inspired personalities are taken literally—and not in a healthy way—as metaphors.

The neurotic behaviors common to more intense episodes may degenerate into specific mental disorders, psychosis being the most typical. As one source* defines it, psychosis is a disorder that causes an individual to experience and interpret reality differently than those around them. These "interpretations" may take the form of delusions or false conceptions. Only one step away from neurosis lies psychosis. During psychotic episodes, the subject does not take poetic images and personas literally, but views them as dogma—that is, as all-encompassing realities.

Another key characteristic of melancholic attack, I note, is the inability to hold physically still. The patient is forced out of bed, to walk to the window, to pace the room, to pray to God that He might ease the suffering . . . all the more difficult for unbelievers. (Here it must be noted there exist cases where a patient subsequently begins to believe in deities. The minute description of such cases is not, however, the aim of this pathography).

Some aspect of physical suffering is truly inseparable from a melancholic fit, which compounds mental debilitation. Four to five hours after the attack's inception it begins, only to remain with the patient for the entire duration. As often with such diseases, in this case the patient endures a fit's intense physical pain through stages of onset, development, culmination—followed by a gradual, though lasting remission—and finally its cessation, which doesn't end the attack but—I must note—marks yet another, entirely natural onset.

As for physical symptoms, the patient may experience tremulations—first yielding are the feet, where tremors moving upward through the legs, ultimately taking over the entire body, then the mind, as such shaking gradually heightens in intensity, to the point where many patient will convert to theistic beliefs.

This disease, cruel as any other disorder, indulgently toys with its victims: a cunning and powerful melancholia, truly merciless. A fit may slowly relinquish its victim, and at times he begins to think that things will get easier—only a sick joke, as after a few minutes or so the disease strikes back with a vengeance, ready to rip to shreds any remnants of pride and self-respect, leaving behind only fear and humiliation. In this the disease succeeds, every time, without exception. Afterwards excessive feelings of guilt effuse the subject, which in turn induce other symptoms often for far longer than the duration of the initial attack(s). This sensation, it could be said, extrudes the pure melancholic sediment from a former state of relapse; this residue the patient is then forced to disentangle, to unravel its parts as you would tightly bound knots, a task which can last one to two week or even longer, depending on a patient's state of health and underlying emotional welfare.

SUCCESS CREATES ITS OWN OPPORTUNITIES

Heaviness. Heaviness in my limbs. My arms, my legs, heavy. Something weighing on me, holding me down. Sounds, signals, squeeze in from outside, ruptures, fragments of conversation. Calm down, someone says, but I can't. Too much stress. Something tortures me, worries me, won't leave me be. I'm lying down and want to get up, but my limbs are heavy, so heavy I can't lift them, tied down. I shout, curse. Calm down, someone says, but I can't, something has taken hold of me and is dragging me under, the earth opens and pulls me down, like leaves, insects, muck, and sucks me in. Dirt into dirt, me and all the rest. They aren't calm at all, those telling me to calm down, actually they're angry, furious and shouting, the channel I hear and see through alone amplifies everything, sharpens everything, agitates me more. I struggle for a while, maybe a few minutes, or maybe only a few seconds, and then I can't fight it off any longer, all will be done with soon, show's over, everything shuts down, I'm sucked back underground, into darkness, a breach, neither here nor there, vacuums pressing at my ears, screaming at me but then I give up because nothing will come to me, all me, all mine, end of the end, sensations hunger, senses, my senses, yours, I want to go home.

Gradually back to my senses, my limbs aren't as heavy, they're lighter, no longer tied down. I'm lying on a bed, next to a greenish wall, or yellow, most likely. Summer. I have no proof for this, but somehow I know it's summer outside the window, to the right of my arm, no longer tied up. In the space where I wake up there are two more beds, someone in each, a person, under the covers something heaves, fidgets. Next to my bed, a life support system, but it's detached, my arm's bandaged, with a catheter in the vein. I want to get up, go out, ask what's going on. No strength. I try to remember. A woman in a nurse's uniform comes in, and suddenly speaks without invitation. No, she doesn't say anything, she looks angry, but I just watch her in silence. She says nothing but signals to me, relays information, and I realize I'm at the Gaiļezers Hospital. I try to figure out what got me here, but can't. My thoughts derail. The detective throws in the towel. I get up from bed, I'm wearing some kind of smock, or gown, I think it's called. It's hard to walk, as if I'm on a tilting ship, and even though the sky is clear outside, summer, sunny, it also looks stormy, and the floor won't stay still, buckles under my feet. I have nothing on under this gown, I'm naked. Where are my clothes? Do I have clothes anymore? I walk to the door, open it, and look out into the hallway. The nurse notices me. Approaches. Then she tells me what happened. I don't like what I hear. She doesn't relish telling me, either. Neither of us is very pleased. A storm rages outside, and no one in our present company is pleased with the current situation. I ask when I can leave, but she says I can't. I have to stay here a while longer. Perhaps I've revealed a distaste or annoyance about these restrictions to my freedom, but at the same time I realize that any struggle is worthless. What fight can you start with nothing on but a hospital gown? Maybe that's why whatever clothes I had have been taken away—to rob me of my willpower and self-esteem. When you're naked, you're powerless against someone in a uniform, or even someone in underwear. I have nothing anyhow. So laughable, everything clothes give us. Drive. Energy. Peace of mind. That's what I'm thinking, because I have no clothes, and without them no drive, energy, peace of mind. I return to bed, which doesn't sway as much as the room. Then I start to think, and, in thinking, to despise myself. I turn toward my neighbor, because its less painful than turning toward myself. I'll look at myself when I leave here. I struggle to recollect what I did before. The last thing I remember—lying on the couch at home. I was texting. Then nothing. Somehow I arrived here. My couch is on the other side of Riga, if I really am in Gaiļezers, though I have no reason to doubt the word of those people who took my clothes and are stronger than me. I peer around the side of the bed. Two people, one young and one old, each in their own bed. Closer to me—a young man, no older than twenty-five. He tosses and turns, restless. In the corner of the next unit over an old man wheezes. Peacefully, even. I listen to his wheezing. I can't see the man's face, but maybe it's not even an old man, even though he wheezes just like one. I pull my blanket over my head and lie on my side. The young man keeps shifting.

Someone is speaking next to him, saying something. He's awake. Then he raises himself up to sit, facing me but without seeing me. He gets on his feet, walks to the door at the end of the room, opens it. Tells the hallway he wants to go home. His gown slides off, so he wraps himself in bedsheets, pulling them around his waist and lifting one corner over his shoulder. He looks kind of like Jesus of Nazareth. A beard, sparse but long. Straight, dark hair. He stands in the doorway, saying something to the clothed people in the corridor. A nurse appears and orders him back to bed. He protests, but she tells him he still can't go home, has to wait, needs to stay. He wants to know how long, and because I also want to know, I listen in, hoping her answer will apply to me too. But the nurse doesn't answer, and instead tries to calm him down, requests his compliance, back to bed. He returns to his bed but continues to fidget. Jesus unpacified. He must deliver his message, but is forbidden to bring it into the world. At present he would rather be walking in the sun, and I too would like to walk in the sun; meanwhile, the old man keeps wheezing. Jesus doesn't stay in bed long. I stare at the ceiling. Jesus gets up, walks to the door, opens it, but goes no further. He's ashamed. Even though his bedsheets cover his nakedness, he won't step further into the hall. Standing at the threshold, he continues to ask for explanations. The nurse returns, angry this time. She threatens to punish him with sanctions if he doesn't calm down. Jesus won't calm down, and I understand him well. Despite all appearances of lying in bed and staring—peacefully, it would seem—at the ceiling. I feel feverish inside and want to scream. But I don't because that would be humiliating. My legs start to tremble, and the nurse practically shoves Jesus back into the room and shuts the door. Jesus keeps asking, he wants to know. Not now, calm down, go to bed, go to bed. Jesus can't, strides from the door to his bed then back to the door, then back to bed then back to the door. I want to go home, he whines. Things are fine with the old man. Perhaps it's the first time in a long time he can sleep in peace, and so he doesn't wake or get up, or whine, just wheezes and coughs. Jesus sits down on the edge of his own bed. A nurse comes in, a different one, maybe not a nurse because she has a different uniform. Jesus jumps to his feet, but the nurse who isn't a nurse, maybe a social worker, approaches my bed. I look at her. She looks at me. I see that she isn't angry, but rather kind. Her eyes are compassionate. She loves all three of us like her own children. She asks if I know how I got here. I tell her I don't. She informs me about the current percentage of my blood alcohol content, which is what brought me here. I don't know if that's high, or very high. Then she asks about my education. I tell her I have a master's degree. Then it occurs to me—is there some relation between my master's degree, my blood alcohol level, and being naked under these covers? In secondary school we used to ask our teachers about the utility of the math we learned, whether we'd ever use derivatives, integrals, or imaginary numbers in real life. When I got my master's degree, I never wondered how useful what I learned would be if I ever woke up naked, strapped to a bed. But maybe, someday, I'll understand. The nurse, who isn't a nurse, writes something in a notebook. Then she says I should seriously reconsider my lifestyle. I want to tell her that every day I think about my lifestyle, the course of life and fate, my state of health, taxes, rent increases, past and former lives. I want to tell her that it's all a misunderstanding. If you give me just one more chance, I can show you how all of this is just one big misunderstanding, I'm not meant to be here, but out there, in the sunlit world, doing things appropriate for someone with a master's degree. I ask when I can go. Soon, answers the nurse, who is not at all a nurse. Jesus, who's been observing us, also wants to know. The nurse will come by soon, says the nurse who isn't a nurse, and leaves. Jesus follows her to the door, goes out into the hallway. Now he's despondent. Someone in the hallway yells at him and he comes back inside, a nurse following him; she shows him to his bed and threatens him with more sanctions. Jesus begs for mercy, because whoever yelled at him wants to hurt him, or so I hear in his voice. The voice of a person who doesn't want to hurt others sounds like that, too. The nurse explains to Jesus that no one's going to hurt him, he knows this, that's why he's here, doesn't he understand, doesn't he know, the nurse wants to know, doesn't he know. Jesus capitulates. You remember your diagnosis, don't you? Don't you know, you're schizophrenic? You can't go out, we can't permit it, you're staying here until you're moved to Tvaiks Street. You aren't going home. She has said something that perhaps she didn't want to. Now all he can do is resign himself. The nurse steps out into the hall, shuts the door. Jesus recedes to his bed, crawls under the covers. Quiet in the ward. I stare at the ceiling, the old man wheezes, Jesus is quiet under his covers. I want to vomit. It's sunny outside, and people with master's degrees are busy doing things appropriate for people with master's degrees. Jesus starts to whimper, so quietly at first that I don't know where the sound is coming from. Now I can hear him sobbing, the covers over his head, which glow golden in the sunlight. He sobs quietly, in short breaths, like a beaten dog. Time passes, the sun shifts, shadows slide past. A nurse comes in and tells me I can go home. I try to get up, but waver on my feet. I want to hold onto the walls in the hallway, but stop myself, as a nurse guides me to where my clothes are arranged on a chair. I'm left alone there. Jacket, pants, shirt. Even a wallet, with money in it. I put on my clothes and look for the exit. Long hallways. I try to gather my strength but get dizzy, my knees won't hold. The path through the halls to the exit seems endless. Walking, I wonder what to do. Do I go home or go to work with M. She'll definitely want to know where I disappeared to the past few days. I'm ashamed. I want to meet her face to face, but I'm afraid I can't stand with my knees straight. I have no choice. I have a choice, but I have no choice. The sun beats down on the concrete pavement outside the hospital.

THE PREMIERE

If I were presented with the chance not to be myself, but to be someone else, and by chance met myself on the street, maybe by a theater while waiting outside for a performance to begin, two tickets in my hands already a little damp from my sweaty palms, since my heart's racing and my blood pressure spiking out of worry that the person I bought the other ticket for might not show or may even join other people or go to another theater, meaning the space next to me will be empty and from the stage the actors will throw glances at the vacant seat, and I'll have to watch the show for two, a far more difficult undertaking than I have the patience or courage for; if I were presented with the chance not to be myself, but to be someone else, I would walk up and stand close, then tell myself, "You scared me!"

ON THE ADVANTAGES
AND DISADVANTAGES OF
OTHER LANGUAGES

I sometimes like to write and speak in languages other than the one in which I usually write or speak. Even what I write here, for example, isn't in that language, but another, which gives me the chance to say what I couldn't or wouldn't want to say in my own language. But problems arise when this language gets mixed up with the other—and not only does the person to whom I began to write or speak lose the sense of which language I'm writing in or speaking, but even I start to, too. In which case: how can I trust myself if I can't tell whether what I write or say is really what I want to have written, or spoken?

A VERY SPECIAL PERSON

I know a very special person and value our relationship very highly. Special because even though you can trust in him, you can't trust him with anything. You can trust most people with a lot, but there are very few you can trust in. That's just how most people are, and I'm one of them. For example, coworkers constantly entrust me with projects, but I can't fully trust in, confide, or really be honest with them. And they don't completely trust in me, either, even when we end up drinking a lot on New Year's or if we see each other at my best friend's house—people just like me, whom you can entrust a lot to.

I sometimes end up feeling very sad and melancholy and want to tell him everything and put my trust in him, but since there's almost nothing you can really trust him with, I never know exactly when he'll be around and available to help me out.

Others might wonder why I'm mixed up with this type of person, a person you can't trust anything with, but I know that no one will really understand my sadness or melancholy the way he can, because he's the person who I can one hundred percent trust in and who will definitely help me out, given he's around; though, like I said, he's almost never around.

There are two reasons for this: on the one hand, no one trusts him with anything because he's almost never around. On the other hand, he's almost never around because he knows that no one will trust him with anything anyway.

If I need any advice, or am just looking for someone to talk to about what's really going on, which does happen, but mostly late at night, I call him up, though he's almost never around, and no one knows how to get ahold of him. When that happens I get really lonely and want to cry because it feels like no one understands me except him—the only one who gets me, the sole person capable of empathizing with me. On those nights I go out in the city in search of him, cursing over how I can't find him anywhere, but all the while knowing that I wouldn't want him to be any other way—not very special— because no matter what he is, nevertheless, the only person I can completely trust in.

SLACKER

Every morning, I wake up nine minutes earlier than the day before. Yesterday, I woke up nine minutes earlier than the day before yesterday. The day before that, the same thing. And earlier and earlier, on and on. If the new sequence can be trusted, then tomorrow I'll wake up nine minutes earlier than today. If this goes on, according to my calculations, after a year I will have gone back a whole fifty-five hours. Or not. I'll just be behind the rest of the world by fifty-five hours. Let's make note of the time: currently it's 7:40 A.M. on December 27th: a year from now, when everyone else is at 7:40 A.M. on December 27th, I'll actually be in the past, that is: at 11:40 P.M. on December 25th. This means that, for me to travel into the past by one year (that's 8,760 hours)—I would have to have lived 159 years. This process definitely has its advantages. Think about it: Let's say I live until I'm seventy-five years old. Let's say I'll die at 7:40 A.M. on December 27th. That leaves me with forty-three years. Not long, but it's enough. But by means of this process, I won't die at 7:40 A.M. on December 27th, 2057, but at

7:40 p.m. on September 18th of that same year. Which in turn means that while everyone else will slowly be getting back from the winter holiday, I'll be enjoying my final second summer through the hospital window, which will be wide open, and I'll breathe in the warm autumn breeze. How I love autumn! But in that moment I won't be seventy-five, but only seventy-four years, since I have an October birthday. But that changes everything, because it all depends on the exact time of my death. Ultimately, it could happen that the following day I will be dead to the world, but will still be alive according to my time, because as noted above though I'll only be seventy-four I'm going to live to seventy-five. Which means I won't die on September 19th, but a little later. Depending on the conditions, I will be granted another seventeen to three hundred eighty-two days of life, during which I will be truly alone, because I will already be dead to everyone else.

FINGERS

Every morning, for three weeks or more now, I've left home with her smell still on my fingers—that is, the index and middle finger of my right hand. That smell, alluring, a little salty, seeps into the depths of my skin, and lingers there almost until the end of the day. Maybe it's this situation people are talking about when they tell their lover: "I don't want to leave! Let me take you with me!" And I do. On my fingers, I bring the scent of her with me. For three weeks running.

As the day goes on, I may forget she's with me, even though almost anything ordinary reminds me of her. For example: when I take a sip of coffee and lift the cup to my lips: through its bitter aroma I discern that familiar scent absorbed by my fingers. Or it's often the case that, if I don't know when we'll see one another again, I purposely refrain from washing my hands, even avoiding handshakes so I don't pass off her scent to anyone else. I don't want to share her with anyone!

Of course, awkward situations follow due to this, like when I set out to shake the hand of someone who wants to greet me;

but it's worth it. Over time I've come up with a solution to this problem, taking her scent on the fingers of my left hand instead, thus avoiding any such inconveniences. Though I soon found her scent wouldn't stay with me during the day like this—not being left-handed, I hold my coffee cup in my right hand, the fingers of which have long lost her scent. Which is why I've since returned to the prior arrangement. So when I left home this morning and walked to the bus stop, her smell, alluring, a little salty, seeped into the depths of my skin—that is, the index and middle finger of my right hand.

GOLDEN HOUR

One of the most wonderful times of the morning, if you're lucky enough to be there, is when streetlights turn on in the city. Let's say you're up because you had a nightmare, or your cat, who hasn't eaten since last night, comes to wake you, so you get dressed in the dark, still cold, shivering with drowsy fever and not yet having made coffee, walk out to the nearest corner store for something to eat and maybe a pack of smokes, because on the way you find only one left in the pack you bought yesterday afternoon, and you're happy with this one cigarette because you'd like a smoke and, well, listen: you aren't fully awake, not yet at least, as you step out to get food for your old cat, seventeen years old already, an old crone you could say, who badgers you like an old lady, and still you haven't done what she asked and she wants to eat, so hurry up, boss, for all those years together, for everything we've been through, for all the pets and sweet meows, get up and go to the store for some chow, I'm going, I'm going because I have no say in this relationship, even though she's got me to thank for almost everything she has—twice this year she nearly croaked, crawling into the corner ready to die, but I told her no, not today you old goat, after all these years of pets and sweet me-ows you can't just leave me, and I carry her out from under the table where she's stolen away to breathe her last, shove her in a carrier and drag her to the vet with the zipper open a crack because I'm afraid she'll suffocate, since how awkward would it be to arrive at the vet's with a dead cat, telling them she must have died on the road, was still breathing at home (that's why I took her there, to be treated, not buried, which I could just as well do anywhere else, in the woods along Iman-ta, for instance). And so I get her to the clinic still alive, and they stabilize her, inject her with vitamins, give her an ultra-sound and an infusion, second time in two years that she's been ready to die; I pack her up and bring her to the vet so she can be revived with injections and live one more year, at least. And now? Now she's alive and well, my little granny, and despite her age is still that shameless cow she was when she was younger. That's why I have to get up at such an early hour and walk to the corner store, lighting my final cigarette from last night's pack, while everything around me is immersed in that wonderful half-brilliance of twilight. Then, suddenly, all the streetlights go out and the neighborhood is washed in twi-light, a pleasant half-dark. The movies call it golden hour, but really it lasts closer for ten to fifteen minutes; long enough for me, at least, to get to a twenty-four-hour grocery and buy food for the cat, but for me—another pack.

THE TELEPHONE

The telephone rings. In the hallway. Where there's also a gray rug. The telephone rings and rings. The sound echoes throughout the whole apartment. The telephone rings, but the boy is six years old. While the telephone rings, the boy suspects nothing. He approaches the telephone and picks up the receiver. "Hello!" Silence hisses in the receiver. "Hello!" he says again. No one wants to talk with the boy. He puts down the receiver and suspects nothing of the horror waiting for him. Time elapses, but he's still six years old. The telephone rings. The boy comes back into the hallway, stands firm on the gray carpet, which is seventeen years old, reaches out, and picks up the phone. "Hello!" he says. Silences hisses in the receiver. "Hello! Say something, please." No one wants to talk with the boy. He puts down the receiver and begins to suspect something. This time he stays standing on the gray rug. Time passes, and the telephone rings. Immediately the boy picks up the receiver. "Hello! Hello!" the boy's voice cracks. "Who is it?" he asks. No answer, only hissing silence. Silence hisses in the receiver, in the hallway, silence begins to hiss through the whole apartment. The boy's afraid to put down the phone. He waits, but nothing happens. He puts down the receiver and doesn't suspecting—because he knows what will happen next. The telephone rings. Again. And again. And again. The boy's afraid to pick up the phone. But he can't not pick it up, because the telephone's ringing, and when a telephone rings you have to pick up. So he does, but his hand, the hand of a six-year-old, shakes. He doesn't say "Hello," just listens and breathes into the receiver. "Who is it? Say something, please. Please . . . Could you please just . . . speak to me! Why aren't you answering?" The boy weeps, tears stream down his face to his mouth, he can taste the salt. "Please, please!" He throws the receiver and pulls out the cord from the socket. He trembles. Suddenly he needs to pee. Time passes and the boy is still standing on the gray carpet in the hallway. He knows he has to plug the telephone back in. He has no choice. He reconnects the telephone. It rings. The boy doesn't pick up the receiver, he crouches in the corner of the hallway, makes himself small, wishes he could creep in deeper, vanish completely. The boy cries and prays to God. But God remains silent, there's only the hissing in the boy's ears, the hissing in the hallway. "Please, please!" the boy screams at the telephone. But the telephone rings. A telephone rings. A telephone rings.

A COURAGEOUS DECISION

Something woke me up, but because I didn't know what it was, I shut my eyes and went on sleeping soundly. There was a boom, a loud sound that woke me, but maybe since I heard it, I had already woken up. I decided to sleep a while longer and listen for any more sounds, but there were none. Judging from how loud the noise was, it happened in my room. The apartment does have other rooms with other people in them, so it must have been one of them because it's not just me here, and besides I had already said goodnight to my roommates earlier, so I concluded that if the sound had only come from my room, someone would have certainly heard it. And so I decided to sleep a while longer and listen if anyone would walk by my room to see what had happened that had surely woken up all the other tenants. But no one came, all was quiet, and I thought maybe nothing happened at all, there was no noise, and if there had been, I had only dreamed it. I tried to remember my dream but couldn't. I couldn't go on sleeping in any case, struggling to fall back asleep, shifting from one side to the other, and though I wasn't afraid I wanted to find out what had woken me up, was there really a sound or had I simply dreamed it, or neither, and perhaps there were no other people at all in the apartment, and maybe I wasn't even in this room, but in some other place entirely, where I'd never been before. I couldn't be sure about that, ultimately, as it was totally dark. But my eyes were closed, I remembered, so I couldn't tell if the darkness was merely before my eyes, or also in the room, which depended, I realized, on whether or not this really was my room or some other place of total darkness. I opened my eyes and confirmed that the darkness was also outside of me.

What had happened? I wanted to know. I don't like the feeling of not knowing what happened. I like to know that I can influence a situation, that my actions have some sway. I feel safer when I do, though I don't really think of myself as cowardly. I'm not afraid of the dark at all. I'm also not afraid of spiders. Or God. But the unknown, I am afraid of that. I like having options. I like to have an escape.

I paused again to listen, but no one had come, no one opened the door, no one turned on the light, no one asked about or explained what happened. Though I'm not one to covet power, I do like having control over people, places, or things. The people in other rooms (if they are still in the apartment, though they usually are at night) aren't manipulative, but I can't totally be sure about that because I don't know them that well—only from the goodnights, the sweet dreams, or the see you in the mornings before shutting the bedroom door to go to sleep. No surprise, then, that none of them have come by to explain what happened. Not only do they not know, they also don't want to explain anything. I was cast out, left on my own. I needed to take some action if I wanted to resolve the situation. If not me, then who. No one had ever done anything for me, and it seemed nobody would this time either. Every person for themselves. But no rush. I turned my head to glance at the clock, but saw nothing, as it was completely dark.

I had to make a decision, I realized: either lay in bed until dawn, when I could investigate and see for myself what had really gone on—what had woken me up—and in the meantime figure out if I'm still in my room and not somewhere else, or instead, take some immediate action. But I didn't know the time, or how long it would be until dawn, so I decided to act immediately, to discover the truth and calm down, though I wasn't really that worried. Just the thought of waiting alone until morning overwhelmed me. I wanted to sleep, but couldn't fall asleep until I knew what had happened.

Two situations played out in my head. First, I'm in my room at home, so there must be a light switch. I could get out of bed, step through total darkness, and once I turn on the light, all will be clear. That would be the quickest, simplest way to resolve things. But that situation entails more risk, because I'm not sure if I'm really in my room, and if I got up and bravely trekked to where the light switch should be and it turned out to be a different room, I don't know what I would run into. Besides, in the second version, if I got scared halfway and decided to go back to bed, I might not remember where it was and would have to stand there and wait until dawn, but that would be very inconvenient, and what's more I could catch a cold and get sick. Even die. So I decided to sleep a while longer and carefully think everything over so I could make the optimal decision for whatever the current situation allowed.

After taking stock, carefully weighing out each argument, I decided to take the greater risk, though in order to lessen my possible entrapment midway, alone in the dark, and to keep from bumping into something sharp or knocking over anything of value if I wasn't in my own room, instead of swiftly getting up and walking over to the light switch I decided to power through the distance, slowly and cautiously, carefully feeling my way by crawling on all fours to where, hopefully, I could arrive at some place where, according to my calculations, the light switch could be found.

Having made this critical decision, I moved onto my stomach, turned in the direction of where the light switch might be, and stuck my right hand into the dark. Sensing nothing there, I let my hand drop: it touched the floor. A wood floor, just like in my room, though this didn't convince me this was my floor because so many other rooms have wood floors. And though I had no reason to conclude by touch alone that this was my bedroom floor, the fact it was wood didn't exclude the possibility that this could be my room. I stretched my left hand forward and brought it next to my right. When I had stabilized myself with both palms on the floor, I carefully began to pull my body off the bed. One after another, I negotiated my palms a little ways forward, and began to feel that my body was nearing the edge of the bedframe. First I drew myself out to my waist. I continued to slowly pull myself forward. My kneecaps cleared the edge of the bed, then onward until only my feet remained on the bed, and I had to exert some effort to hold my weight above such deep and menacing emptiness. I bent my right leg and placed my foot on the floor. Then my left leg. Finally, I had brought my entire body onto the ground. I paused for a moment on my hands and knees. Suddenly it dawned on me that this was my last chance to reconsider without risking everything—the bed was still behind me; if I wanted I could feel around for it and without much effort crawl back inside. I mulled things over. If this really was my room, by crawling on in this direction, there would be no obstacles and after three meters or so I would reach the wall with the light switch. I've never thought of myself as particularly courageous, but I decided to take the risk and began to crawl. I tried to move as slowly as possible, carefully feeling out each centimeter of the floor as I went, as if uncovering some new, unfamiliar territory.

It was when I had gotten halfway there that I began to doubt the legitimacy of my decision, as well as the motivations behind it. I had risked far too much, it felt, and I'm no explorer—no pioneer; I didn't like putting myself in uncertain situations; I didn't climb trees as a kid, it felt too dangerous to me, though once at the park I decided to climb onto the lowest branch and I immediately slipped, tumbled down, and landed on my back so hard it knocked all the air out of me. I couldn't get up on my own, so a neighbor who happened to be nearby and had seen me fall carried me to a bench where I kept gagging, trying to catch my breath.

For all that, I'm still a fearless person—I made my decision, which itself gave me greater strength to venture into the unknown. I set out on my odyssey with an end in mind. Confronting my demons, facing my fears, getting to know my dark side. Yes, I like these thoughts. I'm conquering myself. I'm fracturing, growing, and developing. Breaking boundaries. How many people in this world have gone through what I'm going through? My experience, my life, my choice! I don't have to explain anything to anyone. No more making excuses. I have nothing to be ashamed of. I've grown up, here and now, I'm ready to take responsibility for my actions, for every step I take. While everyone else I know stagnates, I'm moving forward. No, not even that—this is a spiritual experience, something divine. A greater power talks through me, He speaks with each centimeter I advance. My Stations of the Cross! I'm not arrogant, but nothing like this has ever actually happened to anyone else. I was clearly the chose one. Feeling divine inspiration, I slid my palms forward, but started to feel a cramp in my calves. You have to be careful, I told myself.

I tried to calm down, and when I had I stretched my hands back into the dark to continue on my way, when the very thing I had feared so deeply would happen, happened—my fingers touched something. I very nearly started to panic; according to my calculations there shouldn't be anything there, but there it was, I could feel it with my hand, which meant I was not in my room, and so there was no point in going on toward the light switch, because it's not there, and I'll have to squat here until dawn, for hours probably, during which time I'll definitely catch a chill and get sick. And definitely die. Why? Why? Why, when I was so sure, when everything seemed to as I believed, when I had gotten so close, it felt, why, tell me, why is this happening to me? Me—of all people? Had I done something wrong? Hurt someone? It all goes to show, time and time again, that life has no master plan. That we're all insects, less than nothing, a slap of mud in this immense, heartless, unjust universe. You want to do something good, and from the bottom of your heart are ready to change; you worked up the courage, make the effort, but then you're thrown back—helpless and humiliated. How could I have been so idiotic as to believe? How dare I believe that faith would rescue me?

I felt like crying. I almost started crying. My eyes were pressed shut, jaw sorely clenched. This was the end. In despair I kept groping the unknown object. It was angular, but also rounded. It had sharp edges, but a completely smooth surface. It was low and heavy, clunky, in the way, and unknown, threatening, and it was here, where it wasn't supposed to be.

My fingers knocked against something hard, cold, and vertical. I put my palm against it. A wall. I came up on my knees and felt around with both hands. The longer I did, the braver I felt. Now I was convinced it was a wall, smooth and cold. A final hope blossomed inside me—maybe in the dark I had incorrectly judged the distance, and this really was my room, my floor, my wall; if that's the case, then there has to be a light switch on the wall, even though the object I had touched earlier contradicted that. But now I had nothing to lose. It didn't matter if I waited for daylight while crouched on the ground or standing upright, not if certain death awaited me. There are only a few times in your life when you meet death face to face. And not everyone has the strength.

I quickly got up, reached out, and there it was. The light switch. I turned on the light and saw everything. I understood everything. I turned off the light and climbed easily back into bed, where I fell sound asleep.

TO GAZE OUT THE WINDOW

The living room. A couch inside. On the right, mother sits, not far from the window. Her son enters and sits down, but on the other side. He moves closer to her, then turns since regardless of the recent argument they were both so exhausted from, and despite the hurt which had built up over the years, or so he felt, and that he never could resolve no matter how hard he tried, and that's without even considering all the wrongs he'd done her, which she won't forget and which even sometimes keep her up at night, and despite the lapsed promises, odd miscommunications, painful stories, voided stares, and bitter silences, he lays down and rests his head in her lap. The mother places her hand on her son's forehead and continues to gaze out the window.

COLD HANDS

My first thought was—how cold your hands are! Maybe it runs in our family. My hands were warmer, even though I had just come in from outside. I went to see you as soon as I got here. You were lying on the floor, already bathed, in a suit. Who had the time to dress you?

A PATHOLOGICAL CASE

Some accumulate pathologies, and I'm not one of them. But I'm not free of pathologies, either. Really, I'm no hoarder. But what am I supposed to do with these thousands of messages, hundreds of photographs, texts, and so many letters? If I had a fireplace, I would turn out the lights, put on Mozart's "Requiem," and with an expression on my face equal parts desperate and cruel, tear apart my piles of letters and photographs, cards and notes, and toss them into the flames with a solemn gesture. But all these letters, and even the photographs, are digital. What to do?

I could pick up my computer, throw it in the yard behind the shed, and with a face equal parts furious and beaming, swing my axe down on it, smashing it into splinters like a tough log. Though I do need that computer for work.

I could comb through all these files, pick out photos, put every message and document into a new folder, then press "delete," though my face would be expressionless, empty of everything. But what I need is drama.

TWO WAYS IN WHICH THE FOLLOWING SITUATION DIFFERS

The first way in which the following situation differs from another, similar situation, is that I met him—a person I respect and regard quite highly—here, where I figured I would never have met him at all.

The second way, no less important to this situation, but perhaps far more important than the first, is that just as I went to shake his hand and ask him what he was doing here, he took me by the hair and forced me down. I fell to my knees, my face nearly touching the ground, him angrily saying—almost shouting—"Learn humility!"

SLIPPERY ICE

"Brought your kid to work? No one to babysit him?" Tanya, my mother's colleague, was smiling. A pleasant woman, about sixty. I found her somewhat irritating.

"And the beard doesn't suit you," she went on, smiling as before. Over-sensitive, I smiled back. Mom stood by the office door, also smiling. All of us, smiling, but each to ourselves: Tanya, at her ridiculous joke; me, at trying not to look annoyed; and Mom, as if to say, "Don't get upset with her, kiddo!"

My mother hadn't once stepped out of the adjacent room, even though I had been sitting at one of the office tables for twenty minutes or so. I had arrived early, I knew, but my shift ended early; it wasn't yet midnight. Tanya and my mother still had two offices left to clean, and I'd agreed to help them out. Four years since Mom started work here, four years since I had helped her find the job. One night (working a late shift) an acquaintance approached me and asked if she was looking for work. She was—I said—she'd been looking for a while. We drank a glass of Calvados and he gave me a phone number.

He was getting started on his big project, he said. A pretty big project, I thought, because even though I could handle big projects, this project was so big only someone like he could see it through. Maybe I envied him, but it pleased me to think I was able to discern who he was just as much as myself.

That night, I called the number he'd given me. A man's voice answered on the other end of the line.

"How old?" the voice asked.

"Sixty-four."

"How many years' experience?"

"Coming up on ten years."

"Okay. Let's try it. Tell her to be here Wednesday, around eight. We'll go from there."

"Thanks."

"It's what we do."

Once Tanya was gone, I began to clean the floor. Two of us there, alone. The door open, Mom never left her side of the office. Near-silence, only the light hum of ventilation shafts and a sloshing of the mop when I wrung it out in a bucket of murky, soapy water. If I hadn't known she was nearby, I would have felt completely alone. The quiet surprised me, it was almost never like that—Mom liked to talk a lot, telling me about her day at work, her workmates.

"It'll be four years soon, since you started working here. Time flies, right? Doesn't it?" I suddenly regretted saying that. Time flies, what? What the hell made me say that? That's how Mom talks, oh how the time flies, which coming sounded normal from her, or a retiree. But from me? Why was I talking like that? Was it the weight of this silence? I stopped and listened. Ventilation shafts droning. One more try:

"I'm doing good. A lot of work, but that's fine. Great, even; it's good to have so much to do." I wanted to go on, but what to say? I mean, there was I lot could say, but whenever I had the chance to speak (and I did a few times), the power or the patience left me, or everything I wanted to say suddenly lost its meaning, felt boring or pointless. Though an hour ago there had been two things I wanted to share with her. Summoning my strength I went on.

"Another year and you can apply for benefits. It's not super important, but it would be some extra income. As for me, everything's fine. I have a job. And can you imagine, I even have some savings now. Dad would be so happy."

After finishing with the floor I brought the bucket of dirty water out to the restroom. When I got back she was standing by the window, looking outside. Into the dark. All she could see in was her own reflection in the yellowish efflorescence of the hundred-watt lights. Without turning to me, she pulled up the hood of her fur coat.

"Ready?" I asked.

It was late and yet the streets were crowded. The cold had been in retreat for days, the snow thinning out and thawing into wet mush. I'd already said everything I could possibly say that evening, though Mom obviously had no desire to talk. I put my hands in my pockets for my gloves. I found one in my right pocket, put it on. I stuck my hand in the other pocket and found another two gloves there. Also leather, also gray. One the same as the first, and the other nearly identical, but a different brand. I examined all three, failing to comprehend their number. Where had the third come from? Gloves are lost in pairs, one doesn't just get tucked away in a different pocket. Where had I accidentally come across another? I tried to remember. I walked, thinking of gloves and of the people I'd met that day. An older man had come to me that morning—wanting to know if work on his project was going well. On his way out swung around as if in afterthought and asked me:

"How old are you, young man?"

"Thirty-one. Why?"

I could tell by his expression he was thinking this over.

"Good day," he said and left.

I couldn't remember if he'd been wearing gloves or not.

I stopped at the crosswalk and began to wait for the green light; but it was red, glowing red for some time, and while it was red I suddenly grew cold, overcome by a wave of disgust, irritation, and fatigue. I wanted to go home and go to bed as soon as possible. I turned to look for Mom but didn't see her. Forgetting the gloves, I looked for her but saw only strangers passing by. I turned back around, considering the possibility she had already crossed the street and I hadn't noticed, but she wasn't across the street either. Then I started to doubt whether Mom had been with me at all, if we had even left work together or if she had stayed there. This brought me to the question of whether I had actually been by her work at all. Although this feeling was entirely brief and in passing, it felt truly awful. I recalled how a woman had once accused me of harassing her—she'd said that one night last spring I'd come onto her, drunk, apparently. Her accusation had reached me through the grape-vine. I'd been baffled. Me? Harass? When? May? The tenth? What was I doing the night of May tenth? I remembered I'd been home, watching hockey. Yes, a good game that day, we won. I'd never harass anyone! A misunderstanding by the looks of it. No? She swears that it really was me? What would she get out of saying so? But maybe it really happened? I do forget a lot of things. Maybe I'd forgotten this too? But no, it can't be. I was home. Hockey, four to one, our win. We made it to the next round.

That was the feeling I had standing at the intersection. For three seconds or so I thought it over, until I was absolutely certain that Mom had been with me only a few minutes ago, that now she wasn't, and that I didn't know where she had gone. I went back twenty meters or so and paused by the twenty-four-hour grocery. Someone stepped out of the door and nearly fell, sliding on the ice.

I entered the warm and brightly lit store. Before me, a long aisle of shelves. On the floor a cashier was using a rag to scrub soapy mud across the beige tile. How assiduously she worked. I hoped that she'd give me some sign of where to look for Mom, but she just kept wiping the rag across the floor, her head un-moving. I squeezed by her and the shelves, walking on.

Mom was sitting in the furthest corner on the banana crate. It amazed me that, even though there were still people in the store, no one paid attention to this woman in a fur coat sitting on a banana crate. I stood in front of her. I thought I could hear her crying, but realized it was just the sound of the work-er's rag drawing closer. I squatted down. She lifted her head and looked at me. What I did next astonished me. Or rather, what I didn't do—because instead of some loud accusation—like "What the hell, Mom? Why did you disappear? Why are you sitting in this store on a banana crate?"—I squatted down with a composure quite unlike me and asked what had happened. No, I didn't ask, just thought it; I really wanted to know, yet like so many times before I said nothing.

I remembered my father. One day I was sitting in his hospital room while he slept. By then he no longer understood anything happening around him, and I sat like I was sitting now, silent. At the time I had said everything I had to say, about hockey and a trip I was planning with friends for a few days. He slept with his face to the wall and I sat, quiet. I had never felt the need to talk if there was no need to. It used to annoy me, sitting down at a bar after a lecture with other university students, for them to ask: well, Kupriš, is that all you do, listen? I couldn't stand it. But that day, sitting by my father's bed, I felt that not only should I say something, but that I myself wanted to open my mouth so important would tumble from it, and effortlessly. I wanted to give meaning to this moment, because meaning was the first thing lost. Lost like the one who waves, seeing you off at the harbor. You see them from the deck, see them wave, but after that they're no longer waving, and after that they're gone.

And so I decided not to draw things out, but leaned over my father and spoke with great effort.

I seemed to have hit on something I wasn't even aiming for, because Dad recoiled, turned suddenly to face me, and cried out in despair: "Yes, that's right, yes!"—as if I'd woken him with my banal, infected phrases.

By then, the cashier with the rag had approached where Mom and I sat.

"To be honest, I could eat," I said, "Are you hungry?"

"Don't be upset with me, Mom!" I added. "Davai, let's go! There's a small restaurant nearby. It's still open, I think. We could have dinner and talk."

We got up and began making our way to the exit. At the door I heard the cashier call:

"Watch out for ice!"

As we left the store, I took my mother's hand and we slid carefully on wet asphalt toward the restaurant.

BERLIN

A gets off the metro at the Rathaus Neukölln station. It's already dark by the time he gets there. The streets smell like roast meat and asphalt in spring. Old punks and grimy dogs gather around sleeping bags heaped outside a shop. A wonders if he has time to buy something to drink, but then G appears on the other side of the street. A is happy to see him. G smiles, but from this smile A can't tell if G is happy to see him or not. "Any trouble finding the place?" G asks. A says no. He wants to tell him how hard it was to reach the city, but decides against it. A glances back at the punks and dogs by the shop. G looks where A is looking. "Shall we?" G asks. Then they walk. On the way, A glances into ground floor windows, sees a blonde woman cooking dinner in a kitchen, sees furniture abandoned on the pavement. He thinks about how he'd like to be alone as soon as possible. K is waiting for them back home. She greets them warmly and pours coffee. "Thank you," A says. Then all three of them sit at the dinner table. A looks around the kitchen, hoping to notice something. The

ANDRIS KUPRIŠS

coffee pot sits on the table along with a few pastries. "Do you guys have anything to drink?" G and K exchange glances, their chairs suddenly become uncomfortable. "I don't know," G says. "I spoke with D today, he said not to give you anything to drink." A is unpleasantly surprised by D's request, but doesn't say this out loud. What A does say out loud is: "I think D is exaggerating. Why would he say that? What else did he say?" G shifts awkwardly in his chair. "Not much, he just said it would be better for you not to drink." A tries to act as though he doesn't care whether he gets a drink or not. There's no telling how long this conversation will last, but after a while G gets up and brings out a three-liter box of wine. "Not much here, but enough for a glass each." K declines, and so the men pour more for themselves. When A is later asked what he remembers about this episode, he answers: not much. G responds similarly. Maybe they talked some more, maybe not. Maybe K gets up and, politely taking her leave, goes to another room. A sees nothing significant in this because now he feels calm, relaxed. He's arrived in Berlin, finally, and has a place to stay for at least tonight. So when G asks, "Will you be staying with us tonight?" A answers he would be happy to. Then, for the first time, A can tell from G's face that he's happy to see him. A feels satisfied by this, and begins to feel a sense of stability, of peace. Later K returns and asks if the guys want any dinner, she can cook something. A says nothing, but from the look in his eyes he's very happy to see her. G says they plan on going out somewhere for a drink and then a walk, so they'll probably eat out. This answer satisfies K. Later they're out walking through the darkened streets, G mostly silent, A also without much to say. He thinks again of telling G about his adventures getting to the city, but refrains for some reason. The streets are full of people, far more than there would be in Riga at this hour, A thinks. G has promised to show him a cozy bar where there's live music tonight. It's located at an intersection. Inside is crowded. It's a narrow space, and the many people make it even tighter. On the left, a bar, on the right—several tables. All of these are taken, people press close to the bar top. The musicians are in the far corner. "Blues night tonight," says G, while A spots a table opening. "Save us a place, I'll get drinks," says G, and A nods, and a moment later G returns with the drinks. At the nearest table, people are laughing. A dark red curtain covers one wall of the room. Behind it could be another room, A thinks. One of the people at the loud table next to theirs tips so far back in his chair that A wonders if he'd plunge through the curtain if he toppled, disappearing into the other world. A wants to know more about that other world veiled by the heavy cloth. "It's amateur night," G says. "These aren't professional musicians. Once a week anyone can sign up to play." A is watching the singer. There's some anxiety in her voice, a feeling that something isn't quite right. A takes a look around to ascertain if things are all right. They seem to be. A drinks his beer. G drinks his beer. A looks at G, but he's smiling. A doesn't know what that smile means. "How long are you staying in Berlin?"—"I don't know. Maybe I'll move on to someplace else."—"Where?"—"I don't know. I'll stay in Berlin as long as I need to. But I think I'll need to go somewhere else after, maybe France, or Spain." G gets up to order two more drinks. A reaches for his wallet, but

G says he can pay him back later. Thoughts about the other world, hidden behind the red curtain, return to A. Perhaps behind it is another bar, one the same size, or maybe even larger. Different music plays there, the kid tipping back in his chair having long since toppled over and fallen asleep, while A keeps walking the length of the bar's empty rooms, because nobody's on this other side, no one pressing up against one another, no plumes of cigarette smoke, just a floor strewn with cigarette butts and a drunk slumped on the empty bar top. A would walk up to that bar and after a moment a bartender in a white shirt and dark waistcoat would appear, wipe his hands with a towel and lend a friendly ear to what A has to tell. "Are you an alcoholic?" G asks after A takes a drink from the fresh bottle. Because it sounds neither like an accusation, nor a reproach, the question doesn't upset A. It sounds as though G simply wants to know. "Clinically—yes," A says. "Clinically—what does that mean?" "I think it means a doctor would medically diagnose me as an alcoholic. By definition I am, but whether that means I'm actually an alcoholic, who knows. I doubt it. I don't know." A smiles while he speaks. He's ready to continue on that topic, but G says nothing more and asks for a cigarette instead. They both smoke. The people at the next table over smoke. Everyone's smoking. Even the bartender on the other side of the curtain has taken a seat at one of the tables and smokes. He looks over at A, but A doesn't notice. How could he, when they are separated by a thick, dark-red, heavy fabric suffused with the smell of the city?

That night I dreamt of an empty bar and a lonely bartender in a white shirt and dark waistcoat, saw him wipe his hands on a towel, his dark, almost black hair, combed and slicked back, his expression weighed down by wrinkles, though not in an ugly way, he was just doing his job and knew he did it well, and he asked me what I'd have, and I ordered a whiskey on the rocks, and while I drank he stood before me, pressed his hands down on his side of the bar, and glanced somewhat slyly at me. I started to tell him why I came to Berlin, why I couldn't stay in Riga, about the people, places, and things, that pursued me, suffocated me, about the hope to break free, and he nodded sympathetically and refilled my glass. I told him I was aware of the consequences, that nothing crazy would happen if I went away for a while, how it would better not just for me, but for everyone else, too, so that when I returned something will definitely have changed, only I still don't know what, but that's why I came to Berlin, to be alone for a while, clear my head and think things over in peace. Then I looked for the exit, I wanted to go home, but I couldn't find a door anywhere, just red fabric all around me, quiet light, and cigarette smoke. I went back at the bar to ask where the exit was, but the bartender wasn't there, though the drunk had woken up, his ear was bleeding, and he probably couldn't hear very well because he screamed at me instead of speaking calmly, howled about how he knew everything, and though I tried to calm him down and ask what it was he knew, he didn't let me and kept screaming and bleeding: "I know everything! I know everything!"

A wakes up more than once that night with the realization he's not home but visiting, a visitor in a city other than Riga, a different city far larger than Riga. The second to last time he wakes up, he sees a yellowish light under the door and a bluish light in the window, but the last time he wakes the room is bright and the couch has gotten harder overnight. K is getting ready for work and G is making coffee. They say good morning, and getting up, he says good morning, packs his bag, and answers K, thank you but I'm not hungry, because K asks if he wants to have breakfast with them. A puts on his backpack and walks to the door. "Where are you going? You could stay a few more nights with us," G says, but A says he needs to be alone, that's why he's here. He thanks them both and agrees to meet with G again soon. Then he walks outside, where it's sunny and full of shops. It's still morning, so A doesn't need to rush to find a hotel. He checks to see if he has money and his passport; each are in their respective pockets. He walks down the street where yesterday he saw the punks and dogs. They're gone, only empty bottles and sleeping bags left. People walk up out of the metro station. He can smell trains from the cool air blowing out of the tunnel. "Odd," he thinks, "how subways smell the same in every city." He tries to make sense of what gives a subway its smell. In London, in Paris, in New York, metros smell the same: the stench of rubber. It's all he can call to mind. Rubber. He pictures to himself how the trains come and go. His bag doesn't feel that heavy, so he decides to walk a bit. He heads toward Karl-Marx-Straße. After three blocks or so he turns onto a side-street. Bicycles lean against trees, someone walks a black dog on a leash. Moving along he crosses by a small, fenced-in park. He spots a small Turkish shop by the park exit. The shopkeeper greets him when he walks in. Approaching the counter, he asks for cigarettes, a bar of chocolate, and two 100 ml bottles of hard liquor. "Schönen Tag!" the cashier says, and A answers: "Vielen Dank!" He finds an open bench in the park where he can look over the central lawn. Next to two bicycles, two youths lie in the grass. They're kissing. An old man sits on another bench, reading a newspaper. A takes out one of the little bottles, listens to the metal twist cap crack, empties it in two swigs. Then he lights a cigarette and feels good. He thinks of how nothing seems quite as complicated as it had a few days before. He wonders if he hadn't rushed things with his decision to leave. Nothing had happened. No one had died. Everyone was alive. It was all some kind of misunderstanding, which was the right word, yes—misunderstanding. Communication errors. Maybe he had reacted harshly at the others, but they also reacted to A pretty personally. Everyone should just calm down a little. From this perspective, all the better that he'd left. Now everyone can take a breath. When he returns it will almost be summer, and everyone will have forgotten winter like a bad dream. These thoughts calmed him. "But, if I'm already here, I should make the most of my trip," he thinks. Then he wonders how he could do that. He definitely wanted to meet S, with whom he'd studied in London and hadn't seen in four years. S would definitely tell him about his experiences. And S would understand him, no doubt about that. A could use the opportunity to write something. He had brought a notebook and two pens. Berlin has plenty of cozy cafes where he could sit for hours, where no one would interrupt him, look over his shoulder, or drive him away. A could write a story, or maybe an essay. Even better—A could write a book about his experiences in Berlin.

Strolls through Berlin. A personal angle. Autofiction. "That would be great," A thinks, "I'd have a whole book when I get back to Riga. And even if no one wants to publish it, I could always show it to my friends to show them what's going on in my head. That would definitely put this misunderstanding to rest," he decides. Then he decides to look for a hotel. The previous night G had said there was a youth hostel not far away. A finds it. It isn't difficult to find, because it isn't hidden. At the front desk A asks what they have available. A one-person room is available, though it seems expensive. He could also get a bed in an eight-person room, which also seems expensive, but his bag feels heavier now. No one is in the room. Of the eight, two beds are taken. He takes a shower, changes his clothes and shoes. He breaks out the other little bottle of liquor. Takes one swig, then another. Then he takes out his pens and notebook. Leaning against the wall, he decides he wants to write a sentence, but doesn't know what kind of sentence he wants to write. A third swig, but still no sentence. He tucks the notebook back into his bag. A man comes into the room, greets him, approaches one of the beds and lies down with his face to the wall. After a while he turns over to ask A for a cigarette. He gives him one, which the man tucks away in his shirt pocket. A decides to take his passport along. He walks out to the lobby and sits by one of the computers. A opens his email. He's received the following message:

"I woke up this morning at six. Then at seven thirty, then eight. Then nine thirty. Then I lay in bed until ten, motionless. Looking out the window at the sky. White, overcast, no clouds or wind. White like no other white. And for those thirty minutes while I lay motionless looking at the sky, it felt like time had totally stopped. The quiet of the apartment enveloped me. And I heard no cars driving by, no noise from the street, just that silence, and that sky, empty and white. And suddenly I was scared that time really had totally stopped.

Then I got up, drank some water and tried to convince myself to get out of bed. The apartment's still so cold that I get out of bed to goosebumps and a damp sweat that is neither energizing nor restorative. But then I slip into your sweatshirt and sweatpants and feel warmer."

A reads the letter again. Then again, slowly. He imagines the white sky, the bedroom. He knows that sky. He knows how cold that room is. He feels scared then, but shakes off the feelings of fear. Instead he starts to think of food. He closes the browser window, gets up, pays, and goes out. He looks up at the sky: bright blue. Time hasn't stopped here, in this city time will never stop. He considers which part of the city to explore. In the distance, where the road bends, he spots the television tower and decides to head in that direction. He walks only ten meters or so before he remembers his hunger. "I need to take care of myself," A thinks. He notices he's standing by the window of a cafe. He enters. The cashier greets him by the counter. Macaroni for three euros. Fine, A thinks. By the wall is a fridge full of drinks. Water, lemonade, beer, wine. A small bottle of wine for two euros. Fine, A thinks, and he orders a plate of macaroni and gets a bottle of red wine from the fridge, then takes a seat on one of the soft leather seats. The table is brown and lacquered, so that when he tilts his head he can see greasy splotches from previous diners. From the nearest table he takes a napkin and carefully cleans the surface, which doesn't get cleaner, since the harder he presses the napkin down, the more the greasy layer has spread over the whole table. A opens the wine. It tastes great. Not sour, but not sweet. Exactly what he needs right now. He thinks of how he'll drink responsibly tonight, in moderation, eat a decent meal, walk around a little, get some coffee at a cafe where young people hang out at. Self-care. While he waits for his food, he opens his notebook and starts to write:

I made the six o'clock bus to Warsaw. It was two storeys, and because there weren't many people traveling from Riga, I was able to find a nice seat on the second floor by a window on the right, close to the front. When we pulled out, a woman sat down to my left, but when reached the highway and I took out a bottle of white wine from my bag, she decided there wasn't enough legroom and moved to a seat in the back. It took me a while to fall asleep, you know it's hard for me on moving vehicles, but I must have drifted off near the Polish border because the next thing I remember we were parked at the Warsaw bus station. It wasn't even six in the morning. I was cold. D had advised me to find a taxi and negotiate for a set price for a ride out of Warsaw. But I wasn't in a hurry. Where would I rush to in a gray Warsaw at five in the morning? Luckily there was a cafe was open. I had to wait a while. I stood by the counter, sizing up everyone else there. Mostly bus drivers and drunks. The bartender was quick to understand my order. I ordered a beer, a vodka, and two sandwiches. I downed the vodka all at once then washed it down with some beer. Warsaw began to appeal to me, and I even felt hungry.

Polish news played on the TV. Thinking back to Czech class in college, I tried to parse some phrases. Mixed with my Russian and what little I knew of Ukrainian, I succeeded in decoding the message: the news was good. Everything was in order, everyone was content, life was moving along within the norm, quite alright with me. When I was ready to go, I went out to the taxis. I offered ten euros, everyone made a face, but one driver was game. We took off. It hadn't even been ten minutes when the taxi driver started to honk at a truck in front of us, drove up alongside it and said something in Polish to the driver. Your ride is ready, hop on up. At first I didn't want to give him the full ten euros since he hadn't even gotten me out of the city, but in the end I did. I climbed up into the cab. The truck driver had a kind face. "Berlin," I told him; a straight shot, he said. All the same to me. Then we set off, the side of the highway dotted with little apple trees under a light drizzle of rain. Then we stopped, and the driver said I had to get out. He was turning the right, while I needed to go straight. I told him thanks, and was ready to hop out when he leaned toward me holding a ten złoty banknote. "Na kofe," he said. I wanted to say thank you, I had enough money, but I lacked the energy and the vocabulary, so took the money and thanked him. When he'd driven off, I realized I must have looked pretty bad—my soiled jacket, dirty boots. No surprise he took pity on me, he probably thought I was hard up. The road sign read "Poznan 268." A half kilometer or so away I found a roadside shop. They sold beer, sausage, and cigarettes. I had cigarettes, so I bought a beer and a sausage. I sat on the curb out front. A shaggy dog, a black mutt, materialized from who knows where, wandered over to me, sat down a few meters away and stared at my mouth. We looked one another in the eyes and I said: "I'm not giving you any sausage and you don't drink beer. So scram! Out of my sight." But the dog didn't hear, or pretended not to, because instead of leaving it just kept watching with dark, bitter-experience-filled eyes as the sausage moved from my hand to my mouth. Of course, he got some in the end. I don't remember most of my journey through Poland. I must've been asleep the entire stretch after the border, since all I can remember is approaching the city on the highway and somehow not being afraid to asleep in a stranger's car—maybe out of exhaustion, or from traveler's nonchalance, or a fugitive's recklessness. I don't remember the driver's face, or how he pulled over and I got in his car. I remember the border, but then only gray fields smothered by fog. I gathered we were nearing the city from the large road sign on an overpass bearing the name of the airport, which was how I knew, as I remembered the airport from the first time I tried to travel there. In truth, that attempt involved passing by the city, not heading into it but getting out before the turn-off so I could hitchhike further, but that time was the first time I'd traveled like that, I had no experience, just some advice from friends. I hadn't intended on heading into this city, but another, entirely different city, farther south, along a fetid sea with old buildings on rotten foundations, but that turned out differently, and ended unexpectedly, even dreadfully. After many more unsuccessful days of hitchhiking and big setbacks I finally reached the border, which, having traveled all day, lightened my mood, but that went to hell again when I was informed that you're not allowed to cross the border at that location on foot; I needed to turn around and turn down another road which leads to a city where I can lawfully cross, but going back would mean walking another ten kilometers and it was already dark out, near the end of April. I remembered I'd been warned that crossing the border on foot was illegal, though was also told not to lose courage and ask one of the drivers standing in the queue to pick me up and drive me over. And so I did, the queue was long by then, I knocked on the window of each car, no one wanted to, they shook their heads or didn't even look in my direction. I don't know how long I stood there, though I don't think I felt despair, since I hadn't been standing too long when a young woman, traveling alone, agreed to take me over the border. Even though she was alone, there wasn't much room in her car; was filled with cardboard boxes and stuffed shopping bags, so I hopped in the back. I remember how relieved I felt to finally be somewhere warm again, the car was moving forward, and that was all I needed in the moment, because I didn't feel like moving anymore myself. Even my driver seemed pretty sensible, a young woman in her thirties traveling to another country for work. When she heard where I was going she warned me that she could only bring me over the border and as far as the turn-off for Berlin, as that was where she was going. That works for me, I said, the only important thing for me is to be let out at the turn off for the city that had nothing to do with the city which I hope to reach. The woman was kind and smiled, she said that could also be done. Before we crossed the border, still waiting in a long line of cars, she began to ask about me, where I was going, what I'd been up to till then. She knew nothing about the city I had departed from, but plenty about the one I was traveling to. "It's a really gorgeous city, but in decay," she said to me, then cast a glance in the rear view mirror. It seemed like she expected an answer from me to a question that hadn't yet been asked. "Moral decay," she specified, and began to laugh, for so long and so loud that I grew uncomfortable. "Are you a moral guy?" she asked once she'd recovered from her laughter. Until then the landscape outside the window bored me, but now I focused my attention as I tried to spot some road sign or indication that would tell me how far we were from the city, but all I could see was my own reflection in the dark blue window. I asked how far we were from the turn-off to Berlin, but she didn't answer, didn't even look in the mirror. Later she asked why I wanted to travel to the city I was traveling to, and I answered it was because I loved a book a poet had written about it. She wanted to know which poet, so I told her. "You're a sensitive kid," she said, and at the moment my feet were freezing. After a while she slowed down, switched lanes, then switched on her right turn signal. I told her I had to get out, I didn't need to go to Berlin, I wanted to travel on, but she said nothing, turned off the highway onto a sideroad, the darkness outside the window getting thicker, bluer, and my feet—even colder. I said again we'd agreed to let me off somewhere I could hitch another ride, but she said that, as I could see, there weren't any places like that here. Her voice broke, and only then did I notice how agitated she was, how her eyes kept darting to the mirror, how her hand reached for the gearshift at all the wrong times. I was surprised because I should have been the nervous one, and I was, but when I noticed her agitation, a disquiet replaced my fear; maybe we were both afraid, not just of one another, but of something else too, of objective reality or some force majeure. I wanted to tell her to stop the car immediately so I could get out, but she spoke first and said she was stopping and wanted me get out. Where am I, I asked, where are we, but the car had already come to a stop, leaving tire marks on the asphalt, and then she screamed at me to get lost, get out right now, pointing to somewhere on the horizon. "There's the airport!" she barked as I fumbled in the dark for the door handle. In the distance, an immense cloud of light hung over the fields.

Now I knew what I didn't want, now I had experience. Now, when I saw the name of the airport on a large road sign, I remembered this. I told the driver I needed to get to Berlin, no further. "Yes, yes," he said, "I hitchhiked when I was younger, things like that happen, I know, I'll let you off at a gas station."—"Before the turn-off to the city?" I repeated. "Yes, yes, before the city, where else. I'll let you off at a gas station, but I need to drive on, I don't need to go to the city." By then I was completely awake, I remembered the name of the airport, a sign which indicated two kilometers left, and soon his car was slowing down, the yellow outline of a gas station appeared on the horizon, and we turned off the highway. Maybe we shook hands, I don't know why I thought he was so friendly. I wanted to be friendly too and said thank you. He repeated that I was in the right place, that I could definitely get to the city from here, I need only ask someone driving in that direction, and they'd definitely pick me up. It was April, ten years since my first haphazard trip to Berlin.

I entered the gas station shop and purchased two cans of beer and a sandwich. I ate the sandwich, then checked whether I could drink there. I looked over my shoulder at the cashier as the pull tab hissed. He didn't even look in my direction. I considered this permission and drank the beers. They were cold, the sandwich warm. Everything was happening as it needed to, I felt. I sat at a table leafing through booklets, and thought how unusual it was for me to be here, sitting at a table in another country, leafing through booklets in another language. It was far easier to find myself there than I had foreseen, though it also took much efforts so my thoughts wouldn't drag me behind. I set my mind on heading into the city. Time to cruise into Berlin. I walked out of the station and approached the first car in line for gas. I wanted to be laconic. "Berlin?" No, answered the driver, who stood at the pump holding a nozzle. No from the next driver as well; I sensed some distrust in his glance. I patiently waited for another car. A woman pulled in. I tried not to scare her when I walked up, but she was somewhat startled. "Berlin? Nein!" No one travels from here to Berlin, she explained. You stop here on the way out. The people who stop at this station have left the city. I tried to understand what she said. It didn't line up with what my last ride had said. It didn't line up with my plans. My plans had been to leave for Berlin and arrive there as soon as possible. I didn't want this trip to go like last time.

Further off was a parking lot, a lot of trucks there, a lot of drivers. Walking closer, I recognized the language. It wasn't the language of this country, but I understood it nonetheless, and wasn't afraid to speak it. I stood and watched the drivers, waiting for someone to notice me. When they did, I spoke up. They all looked at me, then looked at one another. Then they pointed their fingers—each in the direction he was heading. The city's there, one driver pointed in the direction where I'd just come from. No, it's there, another pointed in the opposite direction. There's the turn-off, the first said, you passed it. Yes, I know, but there's also a turn off further on, another overpass, another said. You're in a bad spot, the first said. The only people who stop here are driving out of the city or past it. I thanked them and walked back to the gas station. I couldn't stand that. The first time I didn't want to wind up in Berlin, but I did. This time I wanted to, but couldn't.

I decided to try one last variant. I entered the shop and asked the cashier. "There!' the cashier said, indicating behind his back. "The city isn't in this direction, or that direction. It's behind me."

I walked outside. I had no desire to ask for rides anymore, I didn't see the point. No matter what direction it was in, I was reaching the city by foot. I sat down in the grass and opened up my bag. If I was walking, I would need different shoes. I took off the boots I'd traveled here with and looked for the sneakers in my bag. If I walked along the highway, the police might pick me up. But there was no choice, I had to walk because I needed to get to the city by evening. I needed to arrive before sunset. I had about six hours. I thought again about the road sign with the name of the airport. The airport was two kilometers away or so, I remembered. How far until the sign itself, who knew. I could also just start walking until I reached a turn-off into the city where I could hitch a ride, but that seemed too big a risk. I decided to stick with what I knew. The road sign, two kilometers, on the right. The airport had to be there, and some form of transport must run from there to the city center. I opened a beer and drank it. Which means that I hadn't drunk the beer while I ate, because there were two cans in my bag, exactly as many I purchased at the station. But maybe I bought three. I went back to walk along the highway. I walked against the stream of vehicles. As soon as I set out I felt terrible, since I was practically looking each driver in the face, and they all could see me. At any moment the police would definitely pick me up, it's illegal to walk along the highway, but I had to walk, how else would I reach the city? Thankfully, a strip of concrete ran uninterrupted along the edge of the highway and had its own greenbelt, which gave me some room. I stared out into the distance, but couldn't see a single bridge or overpass which I could check for the road sign for the airport. I was glad to have drunk that beer, which helped me endure the drivers' baffled and irritated glances. I saw each one of them. Took note of every face. I knew that later I would see them all my dreams, or run into them in the future, if I ever succeeded in reaching the future. But to do that I needed to achieve my nearest goal, to reach the city before dark. Maybe being picked up by a police car wouldn't be so bad—that way I could end up somewhere with access to public transport. That cheered me up a little. The drivers' faces became less frightening. Suddenly, it seemed like everything would turn out okay. Ultimately, no one knew where I was, but that was my goal—to somehow arrive someplace where no one could find me. I walked all the way to the airport. It was painful, nerve-wracking, and took a lot of cunning, patience, and effort. Once at the airport I got onto a bus and then transferred to the metro.

I got off the metro at the Rathaus Neukölln station, exiting at ground level. The streets smell like roast meat and asphalt in spring. It was already dark and not a person was around, even though it wasn't late. G was waiting for me. He must have been waiting for hours, I thought to myself, though that couldn't be the case. We went to his place, had some coffee, and hit the streets. G took me to a tiny, smoke-filled bar with live music. Dark and red. Musicians played, people murmured their conversations. G and I were mostly silent, just drank beer and smoked. On the way back to his place I saw a pack of wild dogs. In the gray darkness I almost took them for wolves. They had gathered by the entrance to a store near G's, scrounging for bits of food and sniffing around in the evening light. As I walked by, the leader of the pack locked eyes with me. I stayed with G that night, sleeping on the couch in his living room. I fell fast asleep but woke soon after, glancing at the clock and realizing I had only slept a few hours. Tree branches swayed on the walls of the room. I watched their movements and felt sorry for the way things had turned out. I left in the morning. G offered to let me stay a few more nights, but I wanted to sleep somewhere else, where I could be quiet and think things over alone. Soon I found a youth hostel in the next neighborhood. It cost more than I preferred but I decided to stay. A few guys were also lodging there. I left my stuff and went out to find a place to eat. Sadly, I couldn't find one. I roamed around the neighborhood, through alleys and main streets, looking into ground floor windows, where I saw a red-haired woman making dinner, but couldn't find a single place where I could eat. Tired, I arrived back at the hostel, but this time from the other direction, though I'd been certain I would return from the direction I had left in when I went out to find somewhere to eat, not from the direction I initially arrived from—the two directions being West and East. I went to my room and tried to sleep. In no time at all someone turned on the light and started to talk to me. He was telling me about his family in Poland and why he came here for work. I got up and dressed, excused myself by saying that I needed a smoke, went out into the courtyard. Students were drinking beer and laughing. I also bought a beer, sat on a stool at the edge of the courtyard, lit a cigarette, and thought about that little apartment of yours, and the second night I stayed with you. It snowed overnight, a soft layer of snow shrouding your windows. How I held you in my arms. I remembered. Remembered. The person who hadn't let me sleep came outside and found me in the courtyard. He had a bottle of wine, and offered me some, which I didn't refuse. Then he began to talk again, but I heard none of it, and even writing now can't recall anything of what he told me. I nodded, staring straight ahead at the cheerful students, blond boys and dark-skinned girls. When the wine was finished, someone said they'd go out for another bottle; I sat there waiting but felt the urge to leave, got up and walked back up to the room where somebody else was already asleep, but I had no trouble turning on the light and picking up my bag, I ran outside, stepping through the lobby where the woman at the register looked at me as though asking why I was leaving since I had already paid for another night, but I didn't say anything since I was already out of breath. I ran out onto the street and kept running onto the main road, then to a side street, I ran past strangers, dogs, old people, darkness had fallen, fallen directly onto me, and I had to sip into a corner store and get a few bottles of inexpensive wine and a small bottle of bitters, but to make the purchase I had to open my mouth and talk with the cashier, who was really nice, if somewhat drowsy, one tuft of his hair stood on end as though he'd just gotten out of bed, but his eyes were peaceful and deep-searching, and he knew what I wanted immediately just as he would know how to caress the breasts of his lover, and so I paid, gathered up my purchase and had a drink right there by the door, while the wolves of Berlin howled and garbage trucks effused the city's blooming air with the stench of rot and municipal chemicals. I found a two-star, five-story hotel and rented a room at the very top, and though I couldn't even get undressed I opened a bottle of wine and fell dead asleep, as if unconsciously aware I needed to rest and preserve my strength for the days ahead. I dreamt I had the title to a small plot of land which before I'd apparently only rented. I'd thought it was communal property, but then it turned out it actually belong to me, if only by undivided interest. Do you remember that little meadow, the one behind the children's library I still owe a fine to for a book of Ibsen's? That place, not far from the brick building with the apartment we used to gaze up at from the street, our eyes shining with tears, dreaming of a life there, wondering if that was the place where we would truly be happy? That's the field I'm thinking of, now

I'm its bona-fide owner. Not the apartment, I know, but the field is ours, even if all we have is the undivided interest.

When asleep, you sometimes feel like something is about to happen. Foresight that's not so much foresight, but more an interval between waking and what has woken you up. A hasn't opened his eyes yet, but knows he's awake. Then he realizes it's daytime. Cooler outside. He lays in bed and thinks of how he's awake, but maybe it only seems that way, and he thinks it's only in his dream that he needs to get up, check the time. His dreams had involved some dispute with unknown editors about the title to an article. So A isn't certain which came first—waking up, or the knock on the door to wake him up. He listens to the sound, but doesn't know if it's meant for him. A sixth of a second elapses until he realizes the knocking's on his door. He rushes to his feet, zips up the pants he'd left on and opens the door. Her hair is pulled back in a ponytail. "Raumservice?" she asks. A's eyes are swollen. "Room service?" she repeats, in English. Five seconds go by between his waking and her second question. "Nee, nein, nein, danke!" A says. "Wasser?" she goes on. Now three questions so soon after waking. "Water?" she repeats, perhaps noting that A didn't understand the first question in German. A tries hard to focus. "I know what Wasser is," he thinks. "I don't need it translated." But now around nine seconds have gone by since waking up. Wasser. When she pronounces the word, he feels overcome by a pleasant coolness, and pictures a lake or an ocean where he would like to swim. Wasser. Then A realizes she's offering a bottle of water, complementary for every guest in this hotel. "Ja, bitte!" He settles back down in bed while the door remains open. He hears activity somewhere at the end of the hallway. She reappears after moment and offers a green glass bottle. He opens it and takes a sip of the wine. He'd like to quench his thirst somewhat, so as to speed up his waking. Outside the window someone plays the trombone. "Like in a horror film," A thinks. Then he makes his bed, double checks if his passport's still in his coat pocket. Sunshine outside, asphalt a brownish color. A decides to try again and walk toward the Alexanderplatz television tower, and sets out in the direction of its spire. He wonders about the name of the neighborhood he's in. He tries to remember the name of the street where S lives. All the streets look the same, they all remind him of places he's already been sometime before. Same trees, same bicycles. A thinks back to the last time he met with S. A was twenty-four, S was thirty-eight. They had finished their last classes, submitted their course work, and were both getting ready to quit London and head back to the cities they were born in. S was clean shaven when A caught sight of him sitting in the corner of a student bar by a window with a view to people coming in and out of the metro. It was a warm summer day. "If you want to be a writer, you have to put in work and time. You can't be a writer from seven to eight on Tuesdays and Thursdays. Eight hours, every day, you need to be a writer; you have to read and you have to write." So S had said one night, both of them sitting on the roadside outside a shop somewhere in South London. A sat across from S. "What are you drinking?" S asked. "A pint of Kronenbourg, I think," A answered. "Stay there, I'll pay," S rose. A also wanted to get up and come along with him, he had some money on him for once, he could afford a few beers, but S was already halfway to the bar. When S returned, they clinked their glasses.

"When are you leaving?" A asked.

"Tonight. Actually I don't have a lot of time today, I still need to pack my bags and pay my landlord the last month's rent."

It was quiet in the bar, the loudspeakers silent, bartenders getting ready for the evening rush.

"What will you do in Riga? Why don't you stay in London?"

"I don't know. It's hard for me here. Maybe I just want to be home."

"I understand. I don't like London either. But if I were you, I'd stay anyway. There are opportunities here. Weren't you interested in Alison's offer?"

"That's all up in the air still. I saw her yesterday, we talked it over, but she said her project still hasn't gotten off the ground and there's no guarantee they'll get funding. The research is interesting, but I'm not sure if I want to do it."

"That wouldn't have to be full time. If you started with this project, you could make a little money, get a little confidence. Then you could start working on what you really want. You could write."

"For whom? And what?"

"That's not important right now."

"Sure, I get it. But still. I could be making a mistake, but I have this feeling, somehow, that going back is the right thing to do. And what about you? You're a father now."

"Yes, I wasn't expecting it. But it's my last chance."

"Are you going back into business?"

"No, no, well not at first. To tell the truth . . . I haven't told you the whole story . . . the last time I was in Berlin, I bumped into a neighbor of mine in the stairwell. Guy around my age, nice person. We got to talking, and come to find out he's planning an opening at his art gallery. He's looking for artists. Later that evening he came over, I showed him my pictures. He liked them, or at least he said he did. I don't know."

"But that's fantastic!"

"Yeah, isn't it? But who knows. Though if I were you . . ."

Three students came into the bar, ordering beer and wine. The two of them glanced at the table where the students were sitting down.

"If I were twenty-three . . ."

"I'll be twenty-four soon."

"Sure, some difference there. If I were twenty-three, I would buy a big duffel bag, fill it with books, and travel the world."

"And where would you go?"

"I don't know, that's not important now. But I'd leave. You're young."

"And you're old?"

A watches the sun as it glides over the facades of five-story buildings. Emerging from a store where he's bought two bottles of hard liquor for later, he looks around for the television tower. When he'd entered the store, the spire had been to his right, but now that he's outside, he looks to the left, to where it should be, but it's gone. Clouds, construction cranes, fill the sky. To the right, a wooded park. "Vanished," A thinks, and opens one of the bottles.

"I have something for you," said S. He opened his bag, took out a book. "Have you read it?"

"Not yet," A answered. "What is it?"

"I wanted to give you a parting gift. Not many people know this one, but it definitely has cult status. It was written by a lawyer from Prague, a blip in history. He wasn't a professional writer, just wrote at night, publishing next to nothing. I found it at a flea market for one pound."

A picked up the book, opened its soft cover. There in English, in fine cursive, was written: "For friend A, from S. London 2006."

"When I was your age, I also had literary ambitions. I also wanted to write."

"You don't anymore?"

"When I wanted to, I wanted to write like him. That's how good this book is. My favorite. I hope you like it."

"What's it about?"

"An insect."

"An insect? Is it a children's book?"

"No, the main character wakes up one morning and realizes he's turned into a insect."

"I'm not surprised no one wanted to publish it. Sounds like a psychotic episode."

Then they had another beer, and this time A paid. Three girls watched A while he stood at the bar waiting for drinks, but none of them seemed interested in him. He didn't notice.

When they parted, A embraced S. Then they went their separate ways. As A turns around now, he sees the television tower. He'll go back home and write something beautiful.

Nothing less. So he thinks, even though currently his mind doesn't work in sentences, but in pictures, so he imagines pages of printed text which, when read, transmit a feeling of beauty. Readers shudder, overwhelmed, tears filling their eyes from such a wrenching encounter. A feels the urgent need to sit down and put what he sees down on paper, or else it all will be displaced and no one will ever be able to get it back again. Along the street A spots a Turkish restaurant; he sits down by the window, but orders some tea beforehand. Having taken out his notebook, he puts his pen to paper. Two and a half minutes go by, but it remains blank. Yet after another moment his hand starts to move, and the ballpoint traces blue marks across the paper. "I switched hotels that night. When I woke up, someone was playing the trombone outside the window. I sat for a while on the edge of my bed and listened. I had called S that night and must have said something. I remember the automatic message on the answering machine: "You have reached S. I can't answer the phone right now, but if you leave a message, I can get back to you shortly." I don't remember what I said, but the phone call lasted a minute and seventeen seconds. To answer your question, I don't know how long I'll be staying here. I figured I won't think about anything today, just spend the day walking around the city. Berlin looks different, not how I remember it from earlier visits, though I couldn't say exactly how. Maybe something in the air, or maybe on people's faces. Maybe the trees are taller, having grown during the years I was gone. I notice new details, but no longer recognize what seemed familiar to me, from earlier. As though here everything doesn't just change, but changes place, finds itself on an entirely different side of the city. As though somebody picked it all up like a snow globe with a holiday landscape sealed inside and shook it so roughly that everything has now settled somewhere else. The Alexanderplatz tower constantly disappears from the horizon, only to reappear somewhere else. Letters on street signs are switched, certain Turks more mustachioed, children in strollers—louder. I wander into a neighborhood, the name of which I couldn't tell you, and find myself in front of a building. I don't know why I feel so drawn to it, I just can't pass it by. I lack the words to tell you what I saw there. Your usual two-story apartment building, lilacs and old apple trees overgrown in the front courtyard, a small gate facing the street, and nearby—a short concrete path, fissured over time, which leads to the outer door. There are many such buildings in Berlin, even some in Riga. Grayish-brown, unassuming. I feel a desire to open the gate, approach the door, knock, and greet whoever answers, maybe a child, or maybe some indifferent retiree, though I have enough sense not to just let myself into some stranger's property. Have I ever told you about the house in Riga I tried for so long to locate? For some time I've noticed how when I get lost in daydreams, moments when imagination takes over whatever's left of my mind, I imagine a house, so beautifully present before me, and feel a pleasure with this vision that's hard to put into writing, but reminds me of something I've experienced and long since forgotten. As is the case with this building, the house in my imagination doesn't stand out in any particular way. When it comes to me I'm always in front of the building, looking at it with a warm feeling, with a desire to step in and visit. I've

never been inside, only observed it from a distance. A vision
I've had since childhood, or so it seems, but the building itself
comes from real I've experienced. I don't know where exactly,
but I'm sure, that if I only thought it over carefully, tried to
remember, I would find my way to it. Maybe a classmate from
elementary school lived there. In all likelihood, I'm sure, it's
somewhere in the woods across the Daugava, in Pleskodāle
or Šampēteris. I haven't speculated much more beyond that,
only visited the place in my imagination, whenever I want to
feel safe or protected again. Only very recently, after certain
events, have I begun to doubt, or judge, or think critically
about whether I can actually find this place, if it really exists.
And yet—if that vision lives in my imagination alone, and
not all in the tangible world, where did I disappear to when I
walked for days in the streets of this city.

These reflections tired me out, and wanted badly to sleep,
probably because I hadn't gotten enough rest at night, or
maybe because I had already drunk one or two bottles of the
wine left over from yesterday, and I was so blasted and
weighed down I feared I would fall over on the street then
and there—and drift into a stern, pragmatic German sleep—
so I chose to continue in the direction where I might find
some place I could pass out if the necessity arose, but sadly I
didn't know in which direction such a place might be, so I
simply started to walk straight ahead, down the street, but
maybe I was heading back, though I hadn't even glimpsed the
landmarks I noticed before, seen or noticed anything, heard
the same sounds or met familiar scents. "I need to rest!" I said
to myself, maybe out loud, but I doubt it, because I don't

usually talk to myself, save for those times when you told me I spoke in tongues in my sleep, which really scares you. I walked until I reached a metro station, went down, and the train was pulling up, whipping the platform into a flurry of ice cream and candy wrappers; hats flew off heads, skirts fluttered up, I sat on a train car and tried not to sleep, even though the cabin pleasantly rocked and it felt nice, but I couldn't shake the weight. I saw other passengers staring at me, I was starting to sweat, I needed to get out of that rubber-smelling labyrinth; my luck returned and in the end I managed to escape, came back to that small park with the field in the middle, where the two youths had laid kissing, their bicycles set down beside them, not far from the bench where the old man sat reading the paper, criticizing them, to himself, for immoral conduct in a public place, and there I slept, not on the field but further away, falling down behind a bush that seemed the most dense and could best hide me from the looks of passersby, commuters, pensioners, and most importantly, the police, and I slept such a deep and heavy sleep, the kind not everyone wakes up from that's how heavy it was, but I did wake and got up, and Berlin was still there, I was in this city, but maybe the city was inside of me, seeping into me, infecting me, squeezing me so tightly in its grip not wanting to release me, even if I wanted to run away, but I didn't, not yet. I called S once again, right after I woke up, but still no answer, the answering machine appeased me, I said that I didn't understand why S was ignoring me, had I done something wrong, said or done something offensive, insulted him or overstepped some boundary of our friendship, why won't you talk to me, I'm not asking for much, just to talk a while and maybe meet up, so give me a call, said A, if you get around to listening to this message, call me back, maybe we can meet up at some point, said A, but as he's speaking into the receiver and his voice trails off, A hears a text notification, he ends the call and checks who's written, and it's G inviting him to meet up that evening. "Concert tonight in Kreuzberg at the club by the canal. We'll be there around 11. Come." All around him a red dark that resembles light as it shines, crimson, reflecting off the sky, encouraging and calming him. A stands, wipes dry bits of grass from his pants and jacket, then feels goosebumps, he checks his pockets, finds cigarettes, but his passport pocket is empty. "Maybe I left it in the hotel," he thinks. He checks his phone again: a little after nine. A feels cold, the heaviness from earlier having returned to his body. Something chokes and burns in his chest, around his lungs. A wonders if he still has time for a meal and a little to drink to get himself back into shape. He tries to figure out which direction to walk in order to find the nearest metro station. He starts off on the small gravel path that is the brightest lit. The station has to be somewhere around here. He walks down into the station, his chest cramping even more, though he's calmed by the notion of finally getting to where he needs to be. He enters the Kottbusser Tor station and heads toward the canal at Kottbusser Damm. "The city has gotten busier," he thinks, he thinks, he considers, he wonders if it's Friday night, but he doesn't know what day it is, or the date. Arriving at the canal he sees a new message from G. His plans have changed, he won't be at the club, he might text where he ends up. A feels disappointed, but decides to check out the show even though it's too early. He thinks he should eat something first, but suddenly his appetite's gone. In the darkness at the edge of the canal, teenagers are smoking weed, fragrant clouds float back from the bridge. A rereads G's message to remind himself of the club's name. He asks if there's a cover. The bouncer says it's still early, so no one has to pay and he can enter. Not a single person there. Musicians are setting up on stage. For a while they start to play, but then they stop, say something into the microphone to the engineer, who pulls a cable. A approaches the bar, a bartender in a white shirt and dark waistcoat asks him what he'll have. A feels as though he's seen this bartender once before, but can't remember where, exactly. This dismays him somewhat. "Have we met?" The bartender smooths back his hair, but says nothing. A orders a glass of wine and goes to sit at a table to the left of the stage. He lights a cigarette, looks for an ashtray. The fragments of music the musicians play don't appeal to him, and A knows he won't stay for the concert. He finishes his drink and goes out. At a corner store A buys a bottle of beer and walks back to the canal to sit on a bench. He opens the beer, looks around. Though the streetlight doesn't shine there, A can see that people are sitting on the nearby benches. To the right several youths, drinking and getting ready start their night. To the left, an old man with a dog have settled down for the night. The man lounges across the bench, the dog—on the ground. A wonders if he should stay in Berlin for the rest of his life. What could he do here, he thinks. He could work in a restaurant somewhere. He doesn't speak much German. He could wash dishes, you don't need to know the language for that. He could make a little money, move in with a punk commune that occupies abandoned houses. They wouldn't ask for much. In return he could bring them leftovers from the restaurant. He'd have his own little room and some peace of mind. The beer here is cheap, I'd have enough money for groceries. What else do I need? These ideas start to appeal to A, but he's finished his beer, and he gets up to go and buy another. At the store he notices some computers installed in the back; he pays for fifteen minutes and sits down at one. A opens his email. He's received a new message, which reads: " I read in the news that a man around thirty tried to kill himself by jumping into the Daugava, and my heart nearly stopped. In my mind I know it wasn't you, but something about the story shook me, instinctually, and now I'm on edge. Something's fucked up big time if that's how I feel again, because for a long time it wasn't like that. I used to feel peace. Not any more, not now. Forgive me for writing, I hope everything's fine with you. That you have a lot going on, a lot of literature, and aren't too sad." A returns to the register, picks out a beer from the fridge, but realizes he'll need to come back. The cramping in his chest is a constant reminder he exists, so he decides to buy six small bottles of hard liquor. The cashier tells him it would be cheaper to buy one large bottle, but A knows what he's doing. He takes his purchase and walks out. Strolling back to the bench, he stuffs the bottles into his jacket pockets: two in the inside pockets, one in each side pocket, one in each breast pocket. Now his jacket's heavy, but he feels protected from any danger, plus he has the beer in one hand for an overture. Returning to the canal, A notices the bench where he sat is taken. Flustered, A wants to turn back, but is standing too close for the person sitting there not to notice A was headed for this particular bench, but doesn't want to sit now because he's noticed a stranger there. The stranger turns out to be a woman, who notices A, then that he's flustered, then grows flustered herself because she also has a drink and also wanted to sit there peacefully. For a moment he examines her face, which he almost can't see. Pretty, with a dark complexion. She scoots to one end of the bench, indicating that he's welcome to down. A considers whether he wants to. He makes up his mind and walks away along the small path toward the bridge. Stopping by the bridge, he looks around; he can't see the bench from here. He wonders why he did not sit. He wonders whether he should go back, but that would be totally awkward. Humiliating. He wants to go back, but can't. It would be better if he went somewhere to eat, he remembers he needs to eat something, he could find a Chinese or Vietnamese restaurant, somewhere with soup, there's lots of fiber in soup, it's a healthy, nutritious food that promotes longevity, improves circulation, digestion, and overall wellbeing; what's more it would mean sitting somewhere and rest in a warm place, thought it isn't that cold outside, by all accounts it's warmer in Berlin than it would be in Riga this time of year, this time, this anxious time as the economy slowly recovers, but his overall quality of life declining, sinking underwater, going to shit, you could say, though it's been shit for a long time now, he's covered in shit and it stinks, and it makes A feels awful, helpless and heavy, emotionally unstable as he physically disintegrates, yeah, you could say so, he feels so sorry for himself, so sorry for all the people crossing the bridge, sorry for all the women he's loved, sorry for all the women he's told he's loved, sorry for his mother, sorry for his father, sorry for G, who bailed, for S, who won't answer his calls, sorry for the Kreuzberg Turks, Afghans, and Syrians, sorry for the Jews of Riga who were shot in the Rumbula forest, sorry for the Jews of Philadelphia, who haven't been in a forest since emigrating from USSR in the mid-seventies, sorry for the Blacks and gays for the injustices they've suffered. A feels so sorry, the world's wound bleeds so heavily that he decides something finally has to change, something radical needs to happen, something out of the ordinary, so he pulls out one of the bottles stashed in his pockets, downs it, and turns back to the bench where the girl was sitting, A is ready for an adventure, A is ready to put his life in God's hands. But the bench is empty, she's gone. A feels so sorry she's not there anymore. But now the bench is free, and he still has a little something in his pockets.

"Warum hast du weg?"

A raises his eyes, and there she is. She's standing right where A had stood when he had first caught sight of her. A is sitting right where the woman had sat the first time she had caught sight of him.

"I don't speak German," A opens his mouth and says in English.

"Why did you run away?" she asks, also in English, but with a sonorous German accent. A slides to one side of the bench so the woman can sit beside him. He'd like to get a better look at her, but doesn't dare to turn his head in her direction. She pulls a bottle of white wine out of her bag, uncorks it, takes a swig, offers some to A. He doesn't refuse. After the hard liquor, the wine tastes sharp and vinegary, burns his throat slightly, but goes down without issue.

"Do you live in Kreuzberg?" she asks.

"No, I'm not from Berlin."

A imagines that she has gray eyes, a pretty small mouth, a slender and somewhat fragile neck, like the branch of a young linden. He can't picture her nose.

" I want to do something new tonight, something radical, something out of the ordinary," she says.

Her voice is low and almost rustling, like thick wax paper. "Redheads often have voices like that," A thinks, then assumes the color of her hair.

"Do you believe in God?" she asks. A loses his courage. He doesn't want to talk about God, he doesn't want to think about God. He thinks about sex instead. He's never slept with a Jehovah's witness before. Religion mostly leaves a bad impression on his sex drive. Then he wonders who might be the more passionate lover—a Catholic or a Lutheran. Catholics are definitely more cautious starting out, but when they let go, they surrender themselves to their pleasure with all their body, heart, and soul. A fails to arrive at any judgment about Lutherans, because he tunes back in to what the woman is saying.

"I'd like to think that I believe in God, but I don't think that God could ever do anything for my benefit, y'know?" For the first time, she turns in A's direction, though he stays put. For a moment she looks at him in profile, then straightens her back and looks out again to where the street lamps on the other bank are reflected in the dark water of the canal.

"Well, it seems to me that God exists, of course he does, he can't not exist, but I'm not certain that he'd be good for me."

She takes a drink, and so does he.

"I went to church today. Usually I don't go to church. No one in this city goes to church. Well fine, some probably do, but I don't know anyone who does, but today I went, I was walking by a church this afternoon, somewhere in Schöneberg. I walked past one, and it felt like I had to go, so I went in. It was probably a Lutheran church, I don't know, it was so quiet there, maybe services are in the evening and in the morning, I don't know. But there was no one there during the day when I went in, only some old ladies. Exactly how I would have imagined it, if I had to guess—a big, cold, empty church with a few old ladies. And one of them said to me: 'Say a prayer!' And I told her: 'I don't know how.' And then she said: 'No matter. Just kneel down and tell him something.' And I asked her: 'But what do I say? What do I pray for?'"

The woman takes her bag in her lap, busies herself as though preparing to get up and walk away, but places it back on the bench, remaining seated.

"I haven't ever really thought about these kind of things. I'm not religious. But today, right now? Today I really wanted God to be there, so I could speak with him. But I didn't pray, then. I sat down on one of the cold, wood benches and put my hands together, but had nothing to say. Then I left. And do you know what I saw? I saw the woman who told me how to pray—she smiled at me. When I walked away, she was smiling at me, so sweetly."

The woman holds the bottle against the light to see how much is left, and it appears empty. A pulls a bottle from one of his pockets and offers it to her.

"Oh, thank you," she takes the bottle. "Jägermeister? You're drinking Jägermeister?" A nods and pulls out another bottle.

"How many of those do you have?"

A opens his jacket like a black marketeer selling his wares at a night market.

"My father was an alcoholic," the woman says. Then for a time they're silent, every once and a while touching their lips to their little bottles. A feels incredibly calm and smiles, but the woman doesn't see this.

"Take my hand," one of them says. So they join hands and don't let go for a long time. They stay seated for a while, then they leave, then they have dinner. They hold hands and keep holding them for a long while, which would be ten hours in Riga, two in Barcelona, but four to six in Budapest. During this time of intimacy they walk the streets, streets dark and bright, cobblestoned and paved, they walk for a long time, or at that's how it feels to them, and not once do they let their hands go, they press them ever tighter, and becoming acquainted again with the firmness of this grip, he no longer recognizes the streets, they all look the same, but then they come to a street and on that street—a building that they stand in front of, where she kisses him and tells him they've arrived. She presses a button on the intercom, from which a loud voice speaks, the door buzzes and they climb the stairs until they reach an open door. Hallo, Schatz, glad you made it, who's your friend? This is, this is, and the woman says, this is Paul, Paul, nice to meet you, is your friend a musician, I like his style, a little scuffed up, no? He works in the theater, he writes children's plays, isn't that right, babe? Oh, the theater, that's wonderful, come on in, what a crowd, babe will you get me a drink, the bar is in the next room, this isn't even everyone, we're still waiting on more people, we want a big party, we want to bring the house down before we move out, our landlord's a real son of a bitch. Paul feels like he's about to throw up, he probably should've eaten something, he looks for the bathroom but it's occupied, he walks through the apartment and find the balcony, luckily empty, and he leans over the railing and vomits, dark acid flying down from the fourth floor, which Paul watches splatter onto the street. At least now he feels better. Now he can look for the bar. He doesn't have to go far, and finds a lot of options there. In order to quell the roiling stomach, he chooses champagne, which he thinks the woman would also like. He uncorks a fresh bottle and finds two glasses. Then he looks around to try and find the woman he came here with, but all he can see are unfamiliar faces, glimmering and sweating before him, sparkling in rosy colors. Standing there a moment he realizes he won't find his sweetheart, at least not for now, and so downs one of the glasses, then the other. The bubbles slide into his stomach, fizzing and doing their work. Then Paul inspects the other available bottles and settles on bourbon, which he pours into one of the empty champagne glasses. He needs to sit down and think things over, but he doesn't see a single piece of furniture where he could. It looks like the tenants really have been getting ready to move, and went so far as to remove all the furniture before the party. Paul flows through the apartment, which is enormous, with so many rooms, high ceilings. People in every room. He moves, walking from room to room, but the rooms never cease, each time one follows after the other and then another, and only after a while this seems suspicious to him, and he starts to consider the possibility he may be walking in circles, though in each new room there are new people, or they seem new to him at any rate, but maybe they've only managed to switch places while Paul has been going in circles, though he can't find the bar again anywhere, and so he simply takes glasses from the windowsills and from the corners of the room, as long as there's something in them, but exactly what Paul only ascertains he drinks from them, and deduces the people around him are drinking whiskey, cognac, a bit of white wine, but rarely red wine. Paul starts to wonder if he should be looking for his new sweetheart, the woman he fell in love with, whom the Lutheran God brought him in union with that evening so as to remedy his thirst for a higher eros, insofar as that's possible on earth. But first he needed to tear himself from this circle and change trajectory. He searches for a hidden passage, a door that normally stands closed, but opens at as soon as he brushes against it. And he doesn't have to look long, the door appears, he turns the handle, and enters another room where he definitely hasn't been before, there's no sound here, only a bed, and someone is in it, Paul takes a step closer to look, but a woman's voice tells him don't come any closer, and a man's voice asks who's that, and the "who" is Paul, and the woman his sweetheart, and the man the one who just kissed her breast and is holding her in his arms. It's okay, it' s okay, she tries to calm him so he won't leave, don't go, she whispers, babe, she says, stay right there, and Paul sits, he squats and falls into a chair, soft and deep, and slides down, and lowers his head, but his gaze stays fixed, forward, level with the bed, he watches how the man caresses her, both naked, both beautiful, and the woman says, my love, I'm here, and Paul wants to say he is here too, but he can't speak, the chair has overtaken his limbs, and the woman whispers to Paul to come closer, but a voice which isn't Paul's protests and says don't, stay sitting and watch if you want, but don't come closer, but Paul also doesn't try to approach, the most ardent love is from afar, for a long time now he's understood this, perhaps that's why he's come here, to repeat it one time more, and she moans, while the man just trembles, and Paul wants to raise his head from the headrest to better see their movements, so they can see that he's paying attention, that he isn't indifferent, he's right there, but his head is heavier than his will to lift it, and even their combined threefold desire couldn't move him, but he sees what he needs to see, and she sees that he sees, and the man's voice grows deeper, more peaceful, the woman's moans louder and more encouraging, which doubles the man's strength and quickens Paul's breath, something is building up, right here in this room, in all three of them, if there really are only three and no one else, in a room growing dense, the heavy atmosphere pressing on vital organs, and the woman's moans aren't as loud now, she pleads and yells for him to stop, but he won't stop, and Paul can't do anything, he's getting hot, his palms are so sweaty they slide off of her neck, which he's gripping tight, and she doesn't scream anymore, doesn't beg, but with broken gestures begs Paul to end her suffering, to do something, and Paul would gladly get up and with a swing of an arm knock the man off of her, throwing him onto the ground, or maybe against the wall, and would bury his other fist into the man's nose but he lacks the strength and maybe even the conviction to do so, the only thing he wants now is to abandon this room, this apartment, this city which has worn him out so much, upset his digestion and burned his throat, and done him wrong, its hands around his throat, or maybe his hands around her throat, he thinks, I think.

I stood in the hallway, my forehead against the door I had just emerged from. There was no one else around, all you could hear was one of twelve or so lamps flickering at the end of the corridor. I held my breath and listened for anything happening behind the door, anybody talking, screaming in outrage, or maybe even whispering in despair. Nothing. I pressed my ear against the door, thinking I could maybe hear something, but heard only the blood pounding in my head. The longer I held my breath, the louder I heard it roar. I took a few steps from the door and looked at the spot of sweat left by my cheek. I wondered why I was still in that hallway and not running away. I wasn't afraid, but I knew, I knew I had to get away from there immediately, because anyone walking down the hall would notice me. I waited for the moment I would feel fear rather than just think about it, waiting for a signal in whatever form it might come. I've never been in a situation like this before, I didn't know what to do. What consequences would my actions have? For a moment it felt like I needed to go back, knock on the door unobtrusively, politely, and take a firm hold of the handle with my sweating palm and open the door. Maybe I could go back, maybe everything wasn't as crazy as I had imagined it, maybe no one noticed what happened, I could return with hardly a sound and soon forget that it had happened, I wouldn't have to worry, no one would have to yell, if someone even was yelling, I wouldn't have to stand here sweating, the light wouldn't have to flicker so violently, it could've actually not happened. Yes, I do need to go back in, or open the door, at least, and take a look. Where is my bag? I had a bag. I had a bag? If I had a bag, then I would have left it inside, and my bag has my notebook in it. No one can see that. Not that there's anything too outrageous written there, but still I don't want anyone to see. If my notebook isn't at my hotel, then it's in that bag, but the bag's in the room, if I didn't leave it at the hotel. I put my head in my hands, pressing my palms to my temples as though trying to keep my head together, so it didn't swell, a feeling I often had when I remembered something shameful, something I felt I had to repent for, yet I wasn't fully certain if I needed to repent for anything, because I didn't know all the details. For three or four minutes I stood there, that is—meaning it wasn't long since I had left the room, but had already forgotten the main details of the scene and its principal actors. I wish I'd been alone, exactly as I was in this corridor. Maybe there was no one behind the door, but I wouldn't know for certain until I opened the door and peeked in. I was ready to do it, prepared for action, but couldn't tear my hands from my head, convinced as I was that no sooner would my palms leave my temples than my head would swell so much it would blow up and explode like a rotten pumpkin. That's why, standing not far from the door, I kept my hands on my head, sweating but still unafraid, and yet anxious in wait for a sign to act. All at once, everything all at once. The next moment I was on the street, wearing a coat and hat which I could have gotten from the cloakroom, though I couldn't remember if I'd been in a cloakroom, I was already on the street, walking briskly ahead. The last thing I remember was standing by the door, hands on my temples, sweat dripping down my forearms into my sleeves, cuffs drenched, but now I'm walking down the street, and between then and now—what happened in between? I don't know. To walk down from the fourth floor I would have had to walk to the end of the hallway where there was a door to the stairwell. Or I could have taken the elevator, but though I didn't re-member precisely, I knew, I definitely knew that I didn't take the elevator because that would have meant waiting for it to come up, and there could have been someone in the elevator, someone I wanted nothing to do with, so then I definitely didn't get there by elevator, but took the stairs. Then, most likely, I forced myself to stop to ask the cloakroom attendant for a coat and hat. It wasn't so cold outside that you couldn't go without a coat and hat, but apparently I could have forced myself to get them, which really didn't require much effort, I didn't have to say or ask anything, just give the attendant a number. I felt in my pockets and found the number. How did I get this coat, I wondered, if the number was in my pocket? Maybe there hadn't been an attendant in the cloakroom at all, maybe she had gone to the bathroom or the kitchen to refill a kettle that she could set to boil in the corner by that little desk she would sit when no one came to drop off or pick up their coats. Then she'd sit at that little desk, perpendicular to the table's edge, one hand here, and the other—on the back of the chair. That's how she likes to sit and observe the hall and glance at the outer door and everyone going in and out. On the table she has a laminated plastic sheet, the kind that used exist back in the day, back when she worked as an attendant elsewhere, perhaps a library. Maybe she had shown up here with a nameplate and everything, maybe she stolen it from the last place she worked. I think the nameplate was scratched up, but how could I know that, the little desk was rather far from the cloakroom counter, and in the darkest corner of the room, for that matter. But I still had the number in my hands, which meant that the attendant had not spoken with me. Most likely I climbed over the counter and took—recklessly—my coat and hat, without anyone noticing, let alone the attendant, who sees everything and knows everything, but says nothing. This encouraged me somewhat, for I knew that if she had seen me take and walk—recklessly—away with my coat and hat, she wouldn't tell a soul, because what happens in her cloak room stays in her cloak room. I strode down the street and had the feeling that everyone passing by knew better than I did what had happened today. I tried to avoid their eyes, to look past them, though hardly had any success since I'm accustomed to making eye contact with everyone who passes by me on the street, sometimes even drivers, if I can. Countless times I had to cross the street, there and back again over all four lanes, in order to choose the routes where I would meet the least amount of people. If I saw that three people were headed toward me on my side, but only one person on the opposite side, I would cross over. I was walking home, I wanted to get there as soon as possible. I imagined someone was already waiting there, somehow, even though I lived alone. No, it's too soon, no one who shouldn't know where I live knows, but they could find out if someone who knows where I live told them. Better to be home than here on the street; safer at home, at any rate. Luckily home wasn't far, I crossed the street once more, then walked across a square where some old men sat at one corner smoking; I was almost to the door when it occurred to me it would be better first to look up at my windows to see if there was any suspicious activity going on. I stopped and saw the old men in the corner of the square staring at me. I took out my phone and glanced at the screen, making a show to myself more so than to the old men that I'd remembered something, then realized I could also have a smoke, since I hadn't had a cigarette in several hours; this would be a good reason not to approach my place quite yet. I sat on a bench at the edge of the square, where young people lay kissing on the lawn in the middle, their bicycles thrown to the ground and old men reading newspapers. And realized then that this would be a good chance to carefully consider what had happened. I tried to calm myself. I took the pack and a lighter from my pocket, then lit a cigarette. Why did I do that, I asked myself. Why this anxiety? From the bench I could see the windows of my flat. The curtains were drawn, just as I had left them going out in the morning, or so they looked from the bench. I may have say there for thirty minutes or so, carefully observing everyone who came and went through the door. Then I realized I couldn't sit like that any longer, I had to go inside. Definitely safer at home. At home I know what's happening. I got up from the bench and walked to the door. Entering through it, I slowly climbed the stairs to my flat. I saw no one on the way, luckily. I carefully slid the key into the lock and tried to turn it as quietly as possible. I opened the door, but before going inside, stood and listened. Not a sound from inside. Only everyday noises, if anything, from behind the neighbor's door. I didn't like my neighbors, though I couldn't say why, precisely. In all honesty I've never really talked to them, only run into them on the stairs a few times, but for some reason I decided I didn't like them. They had never been loud, but even if they had been, I wouldn't be bothered much. I do sleep poorly, in fits and starts most nights, but I've never blamed my neighbors, and even if they were loud and thus could be a reason for my poor sleep, I doubt I would blame them because I've been a poor sleeper since childhood, and I'd never considered that an external cause could influence this. So I heard the noises coming from my neighbor's apartment. That's all. I entered my apartment and promptly shut the door. I wasn't paying attention and I closed the door with too much force and it slammed shut with a crash. I froze and held my breath. Silence. I locked the door, trying once again to turn the key as softly as I could, as though I knew someone was in the apartment waiting for me to come back. I couldn't know this, though I also couldn't be certain that there wasn't anyone there besides me. I walked through the apartment to convince myself I was alone. Walking by the window, I closed the curtains, but left a little crack open so I could look out, but in such a way that no one on the street would notice me doing so. If someone had been looking at my window that instant, he wouldn't know if it had been me who left it open or someone else. I didn't really know what good would come of this anonymity, but it wouldn't be overkill, especially in a situation like now, when what had happened to me is something that I could not have imagined just this morning, when I woke up in this apartment and opened the curtains. This morning, when I got the letter. This morning, when I stood at this same window and read through and reread the letter a few times more. It was still on the table. I didn't need to pick it up anymore to know what it said. I knew what was written there. "I knew something terrible happened the other day when I couldn't reach you. This isn't the first time you've gone dark for a few days, but this time I had an especially bad feeling. I tried to reason with myself, telling myself that you'd only turned your phone off, shut yourself up in your mom's apartment to work or at least try to work, but this narrative kept me calm for only so long. My anxiety came back soon enough, denser minute by minute until it felt unbearable, and I had a full-on panic attack, something I'd never experienced before. At first I paced our empty apartment, trying to tidy things up a bit, wash the dishes, then wash them again. I sat down at the computer to watch some mindless videos online, but couldn't stand that for more than a few minutes. The cruelest part of it was I couldn't tell anyone what was happening to me. I felt so ashamed, in so much pain, really, that talking seemed impossible. And if anyone really wanted to know what was going on I don't think I could have explained it to them clearly. When I couldn't stand it any longer I got ready to go to your mom's apartment, but when I was dressed and about to leave, I reconsidered. I didn't know what would be worse—getting all the way there just to find you unconscious, or to be stuck outside a locked door. So instead of going out I crawled under the covers, still in my boots and jacket, and held my breath. I waited to hear your knock on the door, but no one knocked. The apartment was totally silent. Then I started to cry. The tears fell, and I couldn't hold them back. I cried for so long my head started to hurt, and after a time I must've fallen asleep. I saw you in my dream. Your hair was gray, we had gone out to pay some friends a visit, and everyone was talking about your gray hair, but I didn't understand why they were so interested in it. Then I realized that your hair was gray because we had long since separated and you had been living in another country for many years. And once I understood that you were no longer beside me, even though I was still at the same party. I went to look for you, suddenly the rooms were full of people, the music loud, everyone drunk, but you were nowhere to be seen. While looking for you I walked into this one room, where I didn't find you but some people inside rolling around on a bed in the half-dark. I asked if they'd seen you, and they said you'd just been there, had sat and watched them, but must've left. I went on to keep looking for you but didn't find you. The last thing I remember before waking was standing on a balcony and, even though you weren't there, somehow I knew that you had been there, recently, but I'm afraid to look over the balcony railing, so scared that I wake up. I called work to tell them I wouldn't be coming in today. I can't let my boss see my face swollen like this. And I knew I can't stay home. If stayed here alone, all I'd do is cry more, but I didn't know what else to do. At that moment I must've felt so indifferent to what others would think of me that I thought maybe I'd go see Valdis. If not to talk then at least to find out if you were at his place the night before. I got lucky, because he had almost zero customers, so we holed ourselves up in his office, and I told him everything. It was so good that I told him. You know how he likes to talk, but the whole time I talked he actually listened, looking past me in pensive silence. Then we talked about you. I felt better. I wasn't even angry with you. For a moment I didn't feel anything against you, and that was so liberating, so good. Feeling nothing toward you. Not a thing. Almost as though nothing that's happened over the years had anything to do with me. When I pictured you in my mind's eye, and I didn't feel like hitting you or hugging you. I hoped that I could go on without feeling anything toward you, but the feeling soon returned, and it was there when I left Valdis's cafe and started down the street, and the tenderness came back to me, and the grief came back too, and the overwhelming desire to find you and choke you with my own hands."

Light in the room. A tries to rise from his chair, without success at first, but gets to his feet with his third attempt. He sees a woman in a bed, wrapped in sheets, naked. He walks around the apartment. You could hardly tell there was a party last night. Everything seems to have been just cleaned. Luckily the bar seems untouched, a few open bottles of wine, half a bottle of cognac, six unopened bottles of champagne in a box by the table. A knows what he needs to do. He picks out a bottle of champagne and looks for the bathroom. He turns on the faucet, sits down on the edge of the tub. It's especially difficult this morning to get the foil off the neck of the bottle, but soon he's managed to twist the flap and tear off the shiny paper. He unscrews the wire, the cork is ready to leap out. He grabs it in time so it the bottle won't pop open and spray its precious substance over the bathroom walls. He's done a lot of things, but he isn't ready to add licking sparkling wine off bathroom tiles to the list. For the first drink, A drinks only as much as he has the strength for. Then he carefully places the bottle on the floor so it won't accidentally fall out of his shaking hands. A waits. At first it seems like nothing's going to happen, but as A reaches for the bottle again the first wave comes, and he barely manages to pull himself up over the edge of the sink. The stream of water washes the transparent bubbles down the drain. A takes another drink, this time draining the bottle to halfway. The bubbles tear themselves free again, though he manages to hold them back for a few seconds. And even though they too disappear down the sink, slight waves of warmth appear on the horizon, and A knows he'll have to win this battle if he wants to leave the apartment on his own two feet. A brings the bottle back to his mouth, and this time it isn't as hard to hold down the champagne, he manages for much longer, two minutes maybe, before he slumps over the sink and discharges. But he's reached his goal. His muscles relax, sweat drips, his fingers tremble, the last of the bottle's contents stay down and no longer beg for release.

A returns to the other room, picks up the bottle of cognac and tries to thrust it in his pocket, but the pocket's too small. He wants to take the cognac on the road, he could use it, but he doesn't want to carry it, he doesn't want to tramp around Berlin with a half-empty bottle, but he feels bad leaving it there, where it'll get lost, where someone else will find it and won't appreciate all the gifts cognac can give, throwing it away or pouring it down the drain, and so A decides to drink as much as he can handle, which isn't much—about a third of what's left in the bottle. Along with the cognac, the thought of eating occurs to A, as does an appetite of sorts, A tries to remember the last time he ate. I need to eat something, he tells himself, I said I'd take care of myself, he thinks. Then he remembers how he doesn't want to stay in this city any longer, he's so tired, needs to go home, today if possible, but first he has to remember where the hotel is, first he needs to figure out where he's at so he can figure out how to get out of there.

Later, when asked how he got back to the hotel, A says he doesn't know. He remembers the bottle of cognac, the thought of going home. Yet reliable sources have made clear how he got back to the hotel. He was spotted leaving an apartment on Fichtestraße with a bottle in hand that, after walking a few steps toward Urbanstraße, he hid in a bush, perhaps with the intention of going back later to get it. He never returned for the bottle, though; it remained hidden in the bushes for months, until

October of that year when the property manager discovered it and threw it in the trash. Witnesses reported that A remained standing for a long while at the intersection of Fichtestraße and Urbanstraße, staring into space. Some maintained he stood there for as long as seven minutes, while others were convinced that A stood motionless, if you don't count the swaying, for around fifteen minutes. Following this he seems to have entered a pub at the intersection. He approached the bar, was silent for a moment, but then ordered a shot of vodka and a beer. The bar wasn't crowded, it was before noon so there were only a few customers, not counting the dog. Concerning the provenance of the dog, some have stated the animal's owner was Hilda B. (50), the proprietress of the bar, working behind the counter that day, while others claimed the owner to be Jürgen F. (56), a regular customer who, at the time A entered through the door, was leafing through the day's paper and thus did not notice him. A was, however, noticed by another customer: Ove S. (48), a Norwegian, who had been living in Berlin ever since the wall fell, not counting the six months he we was forced to return to Bergen due to a protracted divorce proceeding. When asked to describe A, Ove replied with honesty and brevity: "Frightened." Reports indicate A entered, ordered his drinks, drank the vodka at the bar and then took the pint of beer in both hands and carefully brought it to a table in the corner by the window, the same small table preferred by customer Stefan G. (44), a London-educated photographer and co-owner of the local Galerie Aperture who often came here for a beer and a sandwich following an exhibition opening. Allegedly, A had begun to place the contents of his jacket pockets on the table, including his mobile phone, cigarettes, crumpled banknotes, dirty napkins, as well as a small notebook and two pens. A wanted to smoke, but couldn't find his lighter, so tucked his cigarette back into the pack. Then he's said to have opened the notebook, thumbed and turned through its pages as though trying to find something. Most likely he hadn't found it, because he slammed the notebook shut with such force that some of his beer sloshed onto the table. He took one of the napkins to clean the spilled drink, then noticed something written on it. He was seen to have approached the bar and showed said napkin to Hilda B, who couldn't understand at first what he wanted, but later, having overcome her distaste for the confused customer, said the place he was looking for wasn't far from there, actually on that very street, just on the other end of it. In all likelihood, A thus succeeded in learning the location of his hotel, at which he replaced the contents of his pockets and drank the rest of his beer, then left the bar. The hotel had been expecting him. This was due to the fact that he had last been on the premises—much to his unfeigned surprise—four days ago, while upon arrival he had paid for only one night. A was said to have asked in surprise where he'd been those four days, to which the lobby clerk had replied, also in surprise: "Wie kann ich das wissen?" When A wanted to go up to his room, but the clerk stopped him and explained that his belongings had been removed from the room and stored in the hotel safe. When the clerk brought him his bag, A began to rummage about in it, while the clerk waited impatiently for the confused customer to leave. When A inquired in a borderline threatening tone where his passport was, the clerk answered that all the items found in the room not under the ownership of the hotel were placed in the bag. "But my passport isn't here!" A yelled, but the clerk threatened to call the police if he wouldn't leave. "Wo ist mein Pass?" A continued to yell. Of the events that followed, this much is known: not having found his passport, A decided to return to Riga the same way he arrived—by hitchhiking. He reckoned he didn't need a passport for that. He was seen entering the local supermarket and purchasing two bottles of whiskey and one of white wine. He opened the wine not far from the supermarket entrance, on a side street called Wissmannstraße. From there he walked to the Neukölln metro station, which is not the same station he got out at upon arriving in Berlin. That station was Rathaus Neukölln. Later, in the police department, A said he went there because he didn't know how else to leave the city, thus he decided to leave in the direction he'd come from, namely, with the hope to reach Schönefeld Airport. He did so by boarding a train numbered S45. At the airport parking lot he attempted to ask a woman for ride on the highway to Poland. The woman didn't react to the request, but entered her vehicle and locked the door. Even I don't know how A managed to reach the highway, though there remains witness testimony, possibly not the most reliable, that he was spotted on Route 113, where he spent a considerable amount of time trying to wave down cars. Following several un-successful hours, having finished the bottle of white wine and begun one of the two bottles of whiskey, he was seen gesticulat-ing and yelling something along the lines of: "Я не донесу. Она погаснет. Я не смогу." Afterward he to have yelled: "Чего тебе надо? Чего тебе, блядь, от меня надо?" Three days later, an issue of the free newspaper for the Brandenburg Metropolitan Region published the following announcement on the lower left corner of page six: "On Friday, May 2nd of this year, in the pre-cinct of Valtersdorf, police received information that a person was lying unconscious along a section of Route 113 between Schönefeld Airport and the Schönefeld roundabout. When of-ficers arrived at the scene, they discovered a young man around thirty years old who had been sleeping on the greenway by the highway, where pedestrian passage is forbidden. When woken by the officers, the man did not know where he was, repeating only that he needed to get home. When officers asked where home was, the man began to curse loudly, but did not being brought down to the precinct. There it was confirmed he was intoxicat-ed, with a blood-alcohol ratio of 2.87% per mille. The young man did not have identification, though it was learned he was a citizen of an Eastern European country and had attempted to leave the country with via hitchhiking. The police informed him that pedestrians and hitchhiking on national highways is illegal."

The police precinct provides him with a thin blanket wrapped in cellophane and puts him in a temporary holding cell with and a hard mattress. He tears off the packaging, covers himself, and sleeps. Four times he wakes. Each time he presses a red button by the door, which opens after a second, and he asks to be released. Three times he's given a firm refusal, and told he needs to sleep it off until his blood alcohol falls below two-percent per mille. Three times he goes back and drifts off. Waking up and pushing the button a fourth time, he repeats his request in despair. This time the police official tells him he will be released if someone comes to pick him up. He requests access to his mobile phone, but the official answers that the po-lice will make the call themselves if he tells them who to reach out to. G isn't able to pick him up at the precinct, but is willing to wait for him at the metro station. They release A's bag, an envelope containing his the money found in his pockets, and a clear bag with the two whiskey bottles—one full, the other nearly empty. Then two officers walk him to the train station, buy a ticket, and hand it to him. A feels deeply moved by this, but the officers feel relieved.

A gets off the metro at the Rathaus Neukölln station. The streets smell like roast meat and asphalt in spring. G keeps quiet on the walk home, and A isn't ready to talk either. A spends the night on the guest room couch. Twice he wakes up, each time rummaging in his bag for a bottle and taking a drink. When he wakes up the second time, it's more difficult to fall asleep, though he's had a considerable amount to drink. There's a storm brewing. A knows the feeling well. He rises from the couch, walks onto the balcony. A warm night. The whiskey isn't working anymore. No matter how much he drinks, his entire body grows stiff, his internal organs are all mixed up—stomach rising up, liver rubbing against his backbone, while his lungs feel sunken, almost as low as his hip bones, making it even harder to breathe. As he stands on the balcony, he notices the same exact pack of wolves he had seen his first day in Berlin. He looks for the leader of the pack, but all he can see are young males. They sniff the air, they press against one another, whining like puppies, then scatter back across the length of the road. Soon they'll range out of sight, onto the next street; A goes back inside, drinks some more, and lies back down on the couch. What follows is not quite sleep, but more a drift from some half-conscious state into something else, landscapes streaming past his vision, animals whispering in his ears. Morning comes, G opens the guest room door, sits down on the edge of the couch, and asks A how he feels. Then he tells A he can stay there until eleven, which is when G has to head out, and when A needs to leave, too. A says he still can't stand on his feet, and asks to sleep here at least until evening, and G says he understands, but unfortunately that's not possible. A points out that K will be staying in the apartment, he won't do anything to her, he just wants to sleep a little bit more, because really, truly, he can't do this, and meanwhile G stands by him, repeats that he's really sorry, but A can't stay longer, only until eleven, then he'll have to leave. "Please, don't be angry with me," A says. "I'm not angry," G answers, then gets up, lights a cigarette and goes out onto the balcony. A can see from the couch how he sits on a stool and stares into the middle distance, his face truly neither angry, nor upset, it doesn't have an expression, not even indifference, perhaps some pity, but even if that came across for a moment, it quickly fades again.

At eleven A gathers all his strength, pulls his bag over his shoulders and stations himself in the hall by the outer door. "Got any sunglasses?" he asks. G goes into the bedroom and returns with a pair with black lenses. "These work?" K comes out from the kitchen and offers A a sandwich wrapped in tinfoil. A has strength enough to smile.

Berlin is a sad city, a melancholy city. Heavyhearted, forever pregnant, forever just about to give birth, but incapable of delivering. But it's not a despondence of old age, or a fully-ripened melancholy. Berlin's sorrow is more typical of youth: bitter, irritating like a pinched nerve or a slight headache on a Sunday morning. They call Paris the city of lights. New York—the city that never sleeps. But Berlin? Berlin is the city of everlasting hangovers. Hangovers by all degrees and gradations: mild nausea between Mitte and Potsdamer Squares, the first symptoms of a flu in Schöneberg, bad food-poisoning in Friedrichschain and Prenzlauer Berg, a bright, fatty delirium in Kreuzberg and Neukölln.

Berlin celebrates its youthfulness—not only those who are young, but also those who qualify as young, whether from unemployment or cirrhosis of the liver. Berlin wants to take it easy, take its time, enjoy the present, seize the day, but this desire has a characteristic inability to shut off the raw nerve that constantly reminds you the party is about to end and the return of a pragmatic Monday is nigh. And yet it never comes, although it's always just a day away, poisoning the entire quiet of Sunday. In Berlin it's always Sunday.

This city, where so many carriers of memory have been annihilated, is haunted by apparitions of the future, recollections of what has tried to happen but never occurred, neurotic displays of normalcy, reminders of labors forever incomplete, of debts never to be repaid. Desperate endeavors to act undisturbed, which makes the anxiety all the more visible. But regardless, everything is real here, somehow. Or at least, more real. A kind of hypocrisy, youthful and innocent, opens the door to something more tangible, more true, even if it's genuine tension, a genuine hangover, a genuine nausea, an unfeigned neurosis.

In Berlin, two cities exist next to one another. For every street, every square, and every park has a double. Empty, ornate rental apartments rise up from overgrown gardens. Whole districts of glass construction are as lonely as Tempelhofer Park. In one and the same place, the living reside with the dead. At every intersection, Wim Wender's angels hold dominion.

Berlin is a sorrowful city, only the sorrow is imperceptible, like heavy metals, which gradually build up within an organism. You could spend days, weeks, months, even years here without suspecting your heart is being weighed down. And then—in an instant—perhaps while washing your coffee cup after breakfast, or maybe biking from Weissensee to Görlitzer Park, or detraining at Bülowstraße, you're struck by the realization that some cruel and inexorable process has already begun inside you and—whether you like it or not—there is nothing you can do to stop or change it.

I managed to reach S. He answered the phone and was happy to hear from me. When I told him I had tried calling him a few times, he sounded surprised. He asked if I was in Berlin. I am, I answered. He asked how long I'd been in the city. I told him I didn't know. He asked when I planned on leaving. I answered that I'd hoped to have left by now, but the city was holding me back. Then we were both quiet. Maybe because we didn't have anything to say, or we were so glad to hear each other that we were momentarily lost for words. I sat down on a bench at the bus station, holding the phone to my ear. S asked where I was, and I answered that I was sitting not far from the Alexanderplatz train station. Then I started to cry, and S asked what happened. I didn't answer, only sniffled into the phone. When I finally got myself together, I told him, "Please, forgive me!" Then S said that he would be at work until six, but around seven he could be downtown to meet me. I told him I'd really like to see him.

I won't recount what happened between the moment I hung up the phone and around seven that evening, when I caught sight of S heading toward me from the direction of the Friedrichshain bridge. That's because I need to save space for what happened after. After that, we sat in some bar, drinking beer, and S said that I looked awful. He asked how I ended up with a bruise on my forehead, but I told him I hadn't known I had a bruise on my forehead. Later, when I went into the W.C., I looked at the mirror. And there it was—a small, vivid blue mark, a little above my right eyebrow, already starting to go black. My eyes were red, my lips dry, my gums—white.

I asked him if I could spend the night at his place. Later we sat in his kitchen. I was really glad his wife and kids weren't home that night. I was convinced that, had they been there, S wouldn't let me sleep in his guest room. I drank straight from my whiskey bottle, meanwhile S gently warned me not to drink so much and so fast because he still wanted to talk a while with me. That's the very reason I was drinking so much, I answered, because otherwise I would start falling apart, I also wanted to stay conscious and talk for a while. S said he didn't understand what I meant.

"I don't understand," he said.

"Me neither," I said.

"Why didn't you call sooner?" S asked, but maybe I didn't fully hear his question, because I didn't answer.

ANDRIS KUPRIŠS

"Did you read the book?" S asked, and this time I caught his question and suddenly understood, so I answered:

"Yes, a while back."

"Did you like it?"

"Yeah, I did," I said, drank a bit more, then went on: "I bought his novel in Berlin. You know the one?"

"Which one? The one about the trial? I like his short stories better. Do you know those?"

"No."

"They're really short."

"Yeah, I understand."

"How did you like it?"

"Never read them."

"I mean the book I gave you."

"Ah," I said, but went quiet. I was trying to concentrate. Then, after a moment I said:

"At first I was pretty skeptical. Yeah, skeptical. I thought it was your typical angry man book."

"Angry man book?"

"Yeah, angry man. Book. You know, where the main character wanders through the world, all forlorn, drinks too much, everyone does him wrong, but he alone knows how the world works."

"Are you sleeping?" S asked, since I had closed my eyes while speaking the previous sentence.

"No, I was just thinking about how the world works."

In the morning S came into the guest room, where I hadn't slept, and said that he had called the Latvian embassy. It was closed, because today happens to be a national holiday and the consulate delegate was in the hospital with her daughter, but she can be there at one, open the embassy, and provide me with a travel documents. I asked him what today was. May 4th, S told me. I tore open the envelope in which the police had stored my money and counted it. In ripping open the envelope I accidentally tore the corners of some of the bills, but S took them regardless and handed me a Berlin-Riga bus ticket he'd just bought online. "Tonight, at eight." I asked him for the time. S answered it was a few minutes after eleven. "In the morning," he added. For a moment I thought about how much time there was in the world. "Too much," I said. "What?" S asked.

I get out at the Riga International Bus Station. The streets smell like abjection and sweaty clothes. Homeless people and dogs are gathered by the entrance to the market. I stand for a second and wait to see if someone has come to meet me, but no one has, as no one is knows I'm here. Then I start moving, walking the streets wide and narrow, cobblestoned and paved, nothing has changed, everything is in its place, exactly as when I left it. People push past me, slide ahead into the foreground. Colors sting my eyes in the heady light.

I take out my phone and type out a message: "In Riga. Can we meet for a second?" After a while I receive a message. "I'm at the café working. Maybe don't come in, call when you get here." When I approach the door, she's already outside, smoking. A jacket covers the roundness of her pregnant stomach.

"You're back."

"I'm back."

"You look terrible."

The cigarette in her fingers quivers slightly.

"What's this?"

"What?"

"This!" I point to her stomach.

"For a friend. She's due soon. We're having a baby shower. Everyone has a belly."

"Can I touch it?"

"It's not real."

"Maybe."

"Maybe what?"

ANDRIS KUPRIŠS (1982) is a writer and translator. He studied journalism at the University of Latvia and holds an MA in Photography from Goldsmiths University of London. *Berlin* is his debut work.

IAN GWIN is a writer and translator from Seattle, Washington. He holds an MA in Scandinavian Languages and Literatures at the University of Washington. His writing has been published in *Drifting Sands*, *Kingfisher*, and *Mayfly Haiku*. Andris Kuprišs's *Berlin* is his first full-length translation.